MW00938158

THE REVERE

FACTOR

CAMP HAWTHORNE BOOK TWO

Joyce McPherson

Also by Joyce McPherson

Books in the Camp Hawthorne series

The Pandora Device

The Dickens Connection

THE REVERE FACTOR

CAMP HAWTHORNE BOOK TWO

Joyce McPherson

Cover design by C.T. McPherson

Published by Candleford Press

Copyright © 2016 Joyce McPherson
All rights reserved, including the right of reproduction in whole or
in part in any form.
ISBN: 1534617728
ISBN-13: 978-1534617728

❦

To Dad,
who taught me to see possibilities,
and to Mom,
who gave me courage to pursue them.

❦

≈≈≈

CHAPTER ONE

≈≈≈

Most of the stuff at Camp Hawthorne is a big dark secret, but secrets are more slippery than tadpoles in a jar. When my friends and I returned home from camp, we tried to hide the psychic talents we'd found there, even from our families. Unfortunately, secrets have a habit of slipping out.

Jayden managed to keep his skills under the radar the entire year of seventh grade until his grandmother, Miss Charlotte, decided to clean out the backyard. Summer was coming, and as she said, "those sticks won't clear themselves." He must've thought it would be easier to lift the pile all at once. I was sweeping my porch across the street Saturday morning and saw the whole thing.

He stood beside his house, lifting brown arms skyward as though catching an invisible Frisbee. His curly head was turned away from me, but he paused to look over his shoulder and flash me one of his rare smiles. I knew something was about to happen, and I leaned on my broom to watch.

He took a step to the side, and a pile of sticks the size of a garden shed floated around the corner of the house.

His whole concentration must have been on that pile because he didn't see the mailman walking up the sidewalk, and the floating mound almost knocked him over. The poor man ran for the street and didn't stop until he reached my yard. By that time, the heap had landed by the curb.

"Did you see that?" he asked, blinking rapidly as he looked back at the stick pile and then at me. He passed me the mail with shaking hands. "Morning, Stella. I think I'll take an early lunch."

Yes, secrecy was the hard part.

I waited for Jayden to appear so I could give him a piece of my mind (as Miss Charlotte would say), but then I noticed the top envelope was addressed to me—from Lindsey! I pictured her as I had seen her last, wearing one of her homemade T-shirts—blue with swirls of purple dye—and a dream catcher necklace of beads and feathers strung together.

I peered down the street to her house, the only one with a new coat of paint. Still no car in the driveway. Her family left suddenly last Tuesday when her great uncle had a stroke. They were his only relatives, and Lindsey's mom said they had to go but they would be back in five or six days. I opened the letter and read:

Dear Stella,

Our phones don't work here in the country at Great Uncle Levi's farm. He is doing worse, and Mom says we have to stay longer and I will miss the

*last week of school. Can you tell the teachers for me?
Also, there's something wrong here, but I can't figure
it out. I'm hoping you will know what it is and see the
solution. Please write back right away.*
    Your friend,
    Lindsey

I stared at the letter and tried to get an image of
Lindsey's problem to form in my mind. Nothing.

An uneasy feeling settled in my stomach, like the time
I drank too much soda at the school picnic. I was
supposed to practice bringing up images of old memories
and flashing them forward. But I'd let the exercises slip.
They gave me nightmares every time. Now I couldn't
bring up even a flicker of a possibility to help my best
friend. No images of Lindsey at the farm, no flashing
forward from her letter…nothing. I knew possibilities
didn't come for silly things, like what to have for dinner,
but this was important. If I couldn't use see them now,
what was the point of having a gift at all?

Jayden disappeared into his backyard again. I
wondered if I should show him the letter, but part of me
wanted to wait until I knew more. I slipped it in my
pocket. If I kept it close, maybe the answer would appear
on its own. It *had* to happen. Lindsey needed me.

I put the broom in the shed just as Ellen rattled into my
yard on her old bike. Grandma had found it for her at a
thrift store, and she liked it better than the fancy ten-speed
her parents offered to buy her. "It makes me part of your

neighborhood," she explained. Ellen could be quite reasonable at times, but today was not one of those days.

She was spitting mad, flicking her frizzy red hair over her shoulder as if to brush off the irritation. "Can you believe that new girl at school? She didn't invite me to her party last night. That used to be *my* group." Her eyes narrowed. "Tell me I wasn't that bad last year."

I was trying to decide if I should lie, and I must have paused too long.

"Okay, I used to be that bad. But really!"

"Nice outfit," I said, trying to take her mind off the party.

"You like it? My mom made the vest. She said it would bring out the green in my eyes." She fluttered her eyes at me, and I had to admit they looked greener today. Being friends with Ellen made me notice things I would never have seen before. Probably good training since I wanted to be a scientist when I grew up.

"Are the others here?" she asked.

"No, Lindsey's still out of town, and Jayden has chores. Come in and help me get the pizza."

I always knew it was time for Camp Hawthorne meetings when Jayden arrived. He was punctual to the second. But Lindsey usually wandered in late, her eyes unfocused behind her blonde fringe of bangs. It seemed strange to have a meeting without her.

The front door slammed, and Jayden sauntered in. "Did I miss anything?"

"Not even the first bite of pizza," I said.

He levitated a can of soda into his hand and took a huge gulp.

"That was a close thing with the mailman," I told him. "He saw your floating stick pile and thought he was going crazy."

Ellen bit into a slice and winced. Her new braces made eating painful, and they didn't help her mood either. "We've got to be more careful," she said.

Her bossy tone made me want to do the opposite, but I knew she was right. We weren't being responsible with our gifts, and I was the worst of all. Lindsey needed me, and I was useless.

I felt the paper in my pocket, worry prickling in the back of my mind, but I told myself it wasn't reasonable to expect results right away. I was just a beginner. I pictured my teacher at camp—Aunt Winnie, leaning forward in her wheelchair to tap me on the forehead. "It's all in there," she would say. I wished she could help me now.

"Don't we have plans for this afternoon?" Jayden asked. "Searching for stuff with Ellen?"

"I've got the perfect place," I said. "The old bottle factory. I got us a metal detector, too."

"We won't need it," Ellen grumbled. "I can see what's underground without it."

"But it will be a cover—in case people ask why we're there."

We biked out to the bottle factory, a gray brick building sitting like a gigantic toad in the middle of a weedy field.

"We're bound to find something," Jayden said, setting the metal detector humming. He squared his shoulders and swung it back and forth, like he was warming up for a baseball game.

Ellen chewed on her fingernail. "I'm not getting anything." At the same moment the detector went crazy.

"Not even this?" Jayden asked, scraping away a bit of dirt and holding up a bottle cap.

Ellen tensed. "No. Maybe it wasn't buried deep enough."

"Try again," I said.

Ellen spread her arms with her fingers stretching toward the ground and grimaced with her braces, looking more like a lightening rod expecting to be struck at any moment. "Nothing."

Jayden walked close to her, and the metal detector kept up a steady clicking. By the time he dug down to a second bottle cap, Ellen had turned pale. "Have I lost my powers?" she asked, her voice strained.

I saw our plans for a fun afternoon evaporating. Ellen sat down and refused to budge. Jayden turned off the machine, and we joined her on the ground.

"I've had this terrible feeling for days," she said. "Last week I lost a shoe, and I hovered over every pile in my room, but I couldn't find it. And then yesterday I thought I'd check out the dirt on the way to school, and I couldn't feel a thing."

"Has anything odd happened?" Jayden asked.

"Nothing at all."

"What about your braces?" I said. "Remember what we read about dowsers using the magnetic forces in the earth. What if your braces block them?"

Ellen squinched up her eyes. "If that's the reason, I'm never going to forgive my mom for making me get these. Who cares if your teeth are straight!"

"How long will it take?" Jayden asked.

"A year and a half," she replied through gritted teeth. "A long year and a half."

"Maybe when we get to camp Mr. Parker will have an idea to fix it," I said.

"Is that a possibility?" Her frown relaxed a little.

I didn't want to admit it was my own idea, so I brought up an image of Mr. Parker with his clipboard and his green bow tie and lopsided smile, but nothing further developed. Defeat again—but I couldn't admit it to the others. "It might be."

We gave up on metal detecting. It was no fun without Ellen. The day was getting hot, and we biked to Jayden's house for lemonade. He filled the glasses with lots of ice and brought them out to the porch on a platter held high above his head.

"Show-off," Ellen said.

He grinned and levitated the glasses to us.

"Just be glad the mailman didn't see that," I said.

"What do we do next?" Ellen asked, looking at me expectantly.

My first plan had fizzled out, but I still had the letter. "I've got something to show you."

She read it and passed it to Jayden, and his jaw jutted out. "You haven't been doing your exercises, have you?"

"They give me nightmares," I muttered. I didn't want to see his accusing look, so I glared down the street at Lindsey's house. The huge tree in the front yard was full of the wind chimes she'd made, and they clanged softly in the breeze. For a moment the house and tree seemed to blur—a sure sign of a possibility. I concentrated so hard that the blood rushed in my ears, but no further images grew from the first one.

"You've got to try harder," Jayden said, and my cheeks flushed red. I knew he was right, but I wasn't going to admit it.

"I'm going home right now to work on it." I strode across the street, my chin in the air.

I spent the rest of the day staring at Lindsey's letter, but nothing came. I finally fell asleep with the letter crumpled on my pillow.

❧❧

I woke up to the chiming of the grandfather clock— two in the morning. Though I kept my window open, not even a breeze stirred the curtains. My hair was damp on my forehead. I needed something cold—maybe a glass of milk.

In the kitchen I sat with the cool glass cupped in my hands and tried the letter one more time. I held it in front of me and concentrated on Lindsey. Lately she was going through a Longfellow phase—toting around a book of his poems and reciting them while she swirled her dream catcher necklace from her fingertips.

The image flipped forward to her waving good-bye from the window of her family's car. Then the picture blurred and took shape again as the car turned at a sign post reading Townsend in one direction and Crowley in the other.

But after that, the image froze. No more possibilities. My brain buzzed with the effort, and I lay my head on the table to rest a moment.

I dreamed I was riding in a car, and my parents were in the front seat. "Stella has to see the possibilities," my father said. He turned to look at me, and in that moment the car swerved and there was the horrible sound of screeching tires and metal smashing. My throat tightened in a scream, but no sound came. I woke up panting for air.

I gripped the edge of the table, fighting against the awful dream. I focused on the ordinariness of the kitchen—the dishes left in the drying rack, the oven mitt with the burned thumb, the loaf of bread by the toaster. At last the nightmare faded.

I let out a shaky breath and climbed the stairs to my room. My dream brought back the old ache of missing my parents. If probing for possibilities only led to nightmares, I didn't want anything to do with them. I still didn't know what Lindsey needed. What was the use of pushing it?

The next day I wrote to tell her I was sorry I couldn't help. I felt guilty, but she would be home soon, and we could talk. Even if I didn't know what to do, camp would be the next week, and Aunt Winnie would help us.

The last week of school flew by, and I expected to see Lindsey that weekend, but her family did not return. She didn't write again either. The day before camp, my letter came back: "RETURN TO SENDER. NOT AT THIS ADDRESS."

❦❦

CHAPTER TWO

❦❦

I couldn't sleep that night with Lindsey's letter weighing on my mind. I watched the lighted face of my clock march through the hours, and worried that I'd let time slip away without doing anything.

I finally got up as the sun rose pink through my curtains and peered down the street at Lindsey's house. Still no car in the driveway.

I made a breakfast of scrambled eggs and cornflakes for Grandma and me, and cut some of the climbing roses from our back porch to put in a vase.

Though I couldn't wait to get to camp, it was hard to leave her. We'd taken care of each other for so long, I hated being apart.

"You sure you'll be okay without me?" I asked as we ate together.

She hugged me and told me not to be ridiculous. "Miss Charlotte's going to visit every day," she said, making her eyes big and round like she did when she was pretending to be scary. Jayden's grandmother had a knack for organizing things, and Grandma wasn't a big fan of the organized life.

11

She'd gotten a lot better since last summer, though. Something happened while I was at camp, and she'd stopped bringing homes bags of newspapers and extra clothes. Our house had become like a real home with meals at the kitchen table and reading together on the couch in the living room. She even began talking to me about my parents, something I'd always wanted. I knew she'd be all right, but I would miss her.

"Lindsey back yet?" she asked.

"No, I checked this morning."

Grandma nodded. "I expect she will go directly to camp from her great uncle's farm."

Miss Charlotte drove Jayden and me to our middle school, where Ellen was already waiting. The old white Camp Hawthorne bus arrived moments later, creaking to a stop with a puff of blue smoke. The seats were almost full, but some kids made room for us near a window so we could wave to Miss Charlotte.

She waved back, and the bus drove behind the school, rattling down Perkins Lane, where the train tracks had been paved over.

"Get ready!" Ellen said, clutching my arm.

The bus picked up speed, faster and faster, and excitement like electricity zipped down my spine. We rocketed through the mouth of Old Simmons Tunnel, and the world went black.

Jayden shouted "whoohoo!" over the roaring of the engine, and my stomach lurched as we hurtled forward. The bus shook so hard I wondered if we'd hold together.

Kids shouted, and the air grew cold. At last we shot around a sharp corner, and a pinprick of light shone ahead. It grew into a round disk of blue sky—larger and larger—until we burst from the tunnel onto a smooth highway running between green hills dotted with cows. A single tunnel teleportation, and we were in a completely new place.

"Almost there," Ellen said, releasing my arm with a moan. "I hope I won't be sick."

Someone started up the camp song—"Camp Hawthorne, dear old camp"—more like shouting than singing, and a mile farther, the bus turned through an arch made from three logs with the camp sign swinging from the top. We followed the twisty dirt roads and rolled to a stop under the frilled porch of Twain House.

It looked just as I remembered it from last year. Bulging chimneys sprouted from the roof, and the black and orange pattern in the brick seemed to weave a chain of magic around it.

The entire bus cheered, but I wanted to be quiet and look at everything again—the dining hall across the driveway, the path leading to the Junction Stone, and the wooded hill sloping down to Aunt Winnie's cabin near the lake. I planned to take Lindsey to see her today so we could get help for her problem. A twinge of guilt tarnished the happiness I felt at being back at camp. It was true I hadn't helped Lindsey yet, but now I would make it up to her.

A figure ran toward the bus, waving and smiling—Ivan, in overalls and a black cowboy hat. He'd grown taller since I saw him last.

I pushed up the window and waved. "We're here!"

He whooped and punched a fist to the sky. "Chocolate chip cookies for everyone." He tossed a bag through the window, and Jayden snagged it and passed the cookies around while we waited for the first year campers to get off the bus.

I took a cookie, surprisingly still warm, and bit into the chocolaty crispness. "Whoa—do you think Ivan used his fire power on these?" I asked.

"I don't think he made them," Ellen said with a sniff. "But I *would* like the recipe." I wondered if she was still annoyed about losing her powers.

Ivan was waiting for me when I stepped from the bus. "Where's Lindsey?" he asked.

"We thought she'd come on a different bus," I said.

He frowned. "This is the last one."

Jayden looked at me, raising his eyebrows in a question.

"Still nothing," I said.

"What's going on?" asked Ivan.

I told him about Lindsey's letter, and his lips puckered in a silent whistle. "No cell phone—sounds like my part of the country. I'll check with Mr. Parker to see if he's heard where she is."

In my mind I saw the tree with the wind chimes blurring—and then an image of a dark tunnel, lined with earth, flashed in front of my eyes.

"Stella, are you all right?" Ivan waved a hand in front of my face. "You turned white for a minute."

"I'm fine," I said, but my knees wobbled. "I think Lindsey's letter has something to do with a tunnel."

"Mr. Parker will know what's going on," Ivan said. "Don't worry about it."

But I did worry. What good was a gift for seeing possibilities if I had no idea what it meant?

Ivan started down the path but jogged back toward us. "Hey, can you look out for TJ? She's new, and I think the strange bus ride upset her."

I remembered how weird it was for us last year when we didn't know about the real purpose of camp yet. "We'll do what we can."

We got our bags from the pile, and Jayden offered to carry them all. He had a trick of floating them in front of himself, like he was pushing an invisible trolley. Even at camp we were supposed to make things look natural. We reached Hawthorne House and parted at the top of the stairs—Jayden to the boys' dorm on the third floor and Ellen and me to the girls' dorm down a narrow hallway.

Joanne was just coming out of our bunk room. With her glossy black hair and long legs, she looked like a super-model. She was one of the older campers, and last year she seemed to bear a grudge against all "newbies" as she called us. She scowled at me, and it didn't look like our second year would be any better.

"Is TJ in there?" I asked.

"Do I look like your social secretary?" If her psychic power was withering people on the spot, we'd have been dust already. I hoped she didn't give TJ the same treatment.

We pressed against the wall to let her pass. No sense in getting in Joanne's way the first day.

We found the new girl perched on a top bunk with her legs curled under her. She was much smaller than the rest of us, though I knew she must be about our age. She had short brown braids and delicate features, and she cupped her chin in her hands as she peered through the window at the green curtain of leaves from the Hawthorne elm.

"Are you TJ?" I asked.

"Yes," she muttered and hitched her shoulder away from us.

Ellen stood on tiptoe beside her. "We know how you feel. Last year was our first time at camp, and everything was…"

TJ twisted around. "It's not what you think." She turned away as though she didn't want to talk anymore, but I climbed onto the bunk and sat beside her. I had a hunch about TJ.

"Things will get better if you give camp a chance," I said. "Come with us, and we'll show you around."

TJ stared at me for a long moment, and I smiled. It seemed to do the trick. She dropped down from the bed, and her frown disappeared.

We walked through the house while Ellen pointed out some of the highlights—the camp store in the front room and the portrait of the old Colonel in the parlor. Outside, she made TJ look up at the crazy roofs that pointed in every direction. "This house is a replica of the House of Seven Gables that Nathaniel Hawthorne wrote about," she said.

I gazed fondly at the weathered gray siding and crooked chimneys. I used to think the house was gloomy, but now there was something comfortable and homely about it.

TJ cheered up completely by the time we got to the Junction Stone, a huge gray rock flecked with silver which stood at the intersection of several trails. "Touch the rock for good luck," Ellen ordered.

Three pairs of hands reached out. I patted the rough stone, warmed by the sun, and heard the familiar hum of bugs and twitter of birds. A slight breeze blew the smell of lake water and pine. It was good to be back.

We decided to run on the smooth path to the dining hall, but a booming voice stopped us in our tracks.

"No running, girls!" He seemed to appear from nowhere—a tall guy with a crew cut and square shoulders. He stooped to pull some weeds from the side of the trail.

I thought he must be a gardener, and I was surprised Mr. Parker would hire someone so cranky. We slowed to a walk, but the gardener pursued us with his handful of weeds.

"You new here?" he said, pointing at TJ. She shrank back and her lower lip trembled.

I stepped in front of her. "This is her first year, but the rest of us have been here before." I hoped if I sounded confident he would leave us alone and go back to his weeding.

"You should know better," he countered. "Next time I see you running I'll be taking demerits from Hawthorne House."

"I've never heard of demerits," I said.

"New program this year," he replied, giving us a stern glare.

TJ looked crushed, but I pulled her after me. "Don't let him bother you—most of the people at camp are nice." I spoke loudly in case the gardener was listening and might take the hint.

"How'd he know we were from Hawthorne House?" TJ asked.

"Probably saw us come down the path," I said. "Five paths meet at the Junction Stone, one from each dorm. They're named for the famous authors who started this place—Hawthorne, Whittier, Longfellow, Alcott and Twain. Our team is called the Thornes, short for Hawthorne, and we compete for points. You'll see the chart in the dining hall."

TJ's eyes grew wide, and I worried we'd overwhelmed her with too much information. I looked back at the gardener, weeding by the path. You'd think he would know better than to scare such a little rabbit as TJ.

We arrived at the dining hall as the gong sounded for lunch. Ivan found us and talked the whole way into the building, catching us up on news about the other campers. Some of our friends from last year, like Karen, Cecily and the boys from Bromley, wouldn't be coming. They had invitations to attend Camp Dickens in England.

"There are more camps like ours?" I asked.

"Sure. You don't think we're the only country with ESP?" Ellen said with a toss of her red hair. But I knew she was just as surprised as I was. I wondered what you had to do to get an invitation.

Ivan had news of Lindsey as well. "Mr. Parker got a letter that she will arrive a few days late. Some kind of family crisis."

I missed Lindsey, but mostly I felt bad that I couldn't help her. Was her great uncle's health the family crisis, or was there something more? If only my possibilities would kick in.

അൃ

CHAPTER THREE

അൃ

After lunch Skeeter gave the announcements. She was the head counselor for girls and had seen us through our first year of camp, which had been especially hard due to Dr. Card and the Human Project. When we got in the way of his plan to control the world through psychic powers, the entire camp had been in danger. I was glad we wouldn't have to deal with him this year.

Seeing Skeeter set my thoughts spinning to Lindsey. She admired everything about our head counselor: the fact she studied creative writing in college, the way she could whistle bird calls, even how she wore her hair twisted in a bun with art pencils. Lindsey had worn her hair the same way every Monday in her honor. "Why Monday?" I once asked, but she just gave me her dreamy look and mumbled something about the moon. That was Lindsey. I wished she was here.

"All returning campers are to report to Alcott House for clean-up," Skeeter announced. Groans came from various tables, but she ignored them. "We've got exciting plans to share with you afterwards. Follow me, everyone."

Alcott House was the smallest of the dorms, a yellowish green house sitting at the foot of a steep hill. Under Skeeter's cheerful direction, we split into teams to clean the old barn behind the house. It hadn't been used for animals in years, but it still had lots of cobwebs and dust. We swept the floor and then brought in platforms for a stage and folding chairs in rows. In a short time the barn was transformed to a fresh and cozy theater.

After camp last year I'd read *Little Women*, and the barn reminded me of the plays the March sisters performed in the book. Ellen must have been thinking the same thing. She stood on the stage and peered into the cool duskiness. "Louisa May Alcott would approve," she said.

I climbed up next to her and breathed in the smell of old hay. "I feel like Jo standing here, ready to perform."

Skeeter shooed us from the platform. "Everyone, sit down," she called. "It's time for our big news."

There was a lot of scuffling and bantering as campers tried to find the others from their dorms. We sat near Eugene, back for his second year as counselor-in-training for Hawthorne House. He wore spiked hair and a black camp T-shirt with CIT in big white letters. He was already craning over the heads of the crowd to see if Skeeter was ready to start. "She's going to announce the camp competition," he growled. "The Thornes are going to rock this year."

At last the room grew quiet. "Welcome back to camp," Skeeter began, and everyone cheered. "I want to introduce our new head counselor for boys. He's returning after a year at West Point. Let's welcome Niner."

A guy joined her on the stage and turned to wave at us. I almost fell out of my chair—the new head counselor was the gardener!

I gave Ellen my best look-of-alarm, but she shrugged. "Maybe he improves when you get to know him."

Niner stood at attention, and when he spoke his deep voice boomed like a bullhorn. "It's great to be back. We have new plans for this year, and we're starting with a surprise." He paused for a moment, and the audience seemed to hold its breath. "A primitive camp-out."

"What's that?" Ellen hissed.

Eugene's eyes glowed. "Primitive camping is the best. You carry your tent, dig your own latrine, and cook all your food over an open fire."

"Where does the fire come from?" Ellen asked, squinting at him.

"We gather our firewood."

"Hmm, sounds like the opposite of fun."

But Jayden muttered something to her, and she brightened right away. He was probably reminding her of his stick-collecting abilities.

Niner continued in his megaphone voice. "This will be a solid opportunity for the new campers to discover their gifts. Mr. Parker is talking with them now, so do what you can to help them adjust." He walked off the stage, and the campers erupted in talk.

I caught Eugene by the arm as he was about to take off toward the stage area. "What do you know about Niner?" I asked. The others gathered around. I suspect they were as curious as I was.

"He was the Fellows' CIT when I came, and he's a real stickler for rules, so be careful."

"What's his gift?"

Eugene looked at me strangely. "I think he'd prefer you learn that for yourself. Just remember to follow the rules," he added, and jogged off in the direction of Niner.

"Are there rules at Camp Hawthorne?" Ivan asked.

I giggled because he was the only person I knew who could go through life without knowing things like that.

"Sure," Jayden said. "No electronic devices."

"No running on the trails," Ellen said. "No horseplay in the lake."

Ivan tilted back his cowboy hat. "My Uncle George was strict like that, and boy, did we have fun with him--"

Ellen shook her head at him. "You aren't planning to get in trouble, are you?"

He opened his eyes in a look of innocence that wouldn't fool his grandmother.

"We've already had a run-in with Niner," I said. "Which reminds me—we need to check on TJ and see how she's taking the news."

We found her at the dining hall, standing under a tree with an Asian boy, both of them looking bewildered. She rushed up to us. "Is it true what Mr. Parker said?

Hawthorne and his friends started this camp for kids with psychic powers?"

For an answer, Ivan grinned and held up his hands, lighting all ten fingers.

TJ gasped and jumped back, but the boy surged forward. "Awesome!" He wore round glasses and came in close to get a better look. "Can you teach me to do that?"

"Naw, everyone's gift is different," Ivan said. "You'll have to find your own powers." He turned to us. "Everyone, this is the rest of my team—Roy and TJ."

TJ sat down on the ground.

"You okay?" I asked her.

"Everything's just so strange." She swallowed, like she was willing herself not to cry.

Jayden joined us, and TJ gave a yelp of recognition. "I met you at Ivan's house," she said.

Jayden's dad had taken him to visit during one of his business trips, which was the only way to keep in touch since Ivan's family didn't have electricity or phone.

"I remember you," Jayden replied. "You're the one who fell out of the apple tree."

TJ blushed. "I couldn't believe you caught me."

He shrugged. "I was just using my skills."

Her eyes widened as she put it all together. She whirled on Ivan. "That's why you're so good at starting bonfires."

He winked. "Now you get it."

TJ and Roy wanted to know everyone's gift, and it was dinnertime before we answered all their questions. Roy was a funny kid—he had a habit of repeating everything we told him, like he was committing it to memory. I figured it was the way he dealt with nerves.

Our traditional first night dinner was clam chowder—creamy white with lumps of potatoes and clams. I breathed in the briny smell, and a shivery feeling of belonging traveled all the way to my toes. I'd come a long way since that same dinner a year ago when I'd worried my invitation was a mistake. I understood why TJ sat so quietly through the meal, barely touching her food. I wished I could convince her everything would work out, but some things you have to learn for yourself.

I sipped the steaming chowder from my spoon. "This is even better than last year," I said.

"We've got a new cook," Jayden said. "Someone who also paints."

"Sarah!"

Jayden nodded. "I told her we'd visit after dinner."

Ellen and I pushed away our bowls. "We're ready now."

Sarah was lifting chocolate cakes from the oven when we trooped into the kitchen. Her eyebrows rose all the way to her orange headscarf, and she whipped off her silver oven mitts to envelope us in a group hug. She was the tallest woman I'd ever met, and with her ebony skin and bright dresses, she was easily the most impressive. "Creating" was her gift, and she not only painted pictures, but designed her own fabric and clothing. Today she wore a white chef's apron over a flowing gown with orange and brown geometric shapes.

"Look how you've grown," she said when she finally released us. "Jayden must be four inches taller, and Stella, that braid suits you." I'd let my hair grow longer this year and it was easier to control the general bushiness with one long braid.

Ellen smiled, and Sarah jumped back in mock surprise. "My goodness, what happened to your teeth?"

"I got braces," she muttered, clamping her mouth shut with a frown.

Sarah shook her head. "Any effects?"

"How'd you know?"

"I had braces at your age, and I couldn't paint anything but fruit scenes for the entire two years."

"Do you know how to fix it?" Ellen asked.

"If I did, I'd tell you, honey, but don't let it keep you down. Try to find another gift."

"Can I do that?"

"Sure, lots of people have two gifts."

"Like cooking?" Ellen asked.

"Why not? Come see me when you can, and we'll whip up something together."

I lingered behind after the others returned to our table. I'd been looking for Mr. Parker and Aunt Winnie all day, with no luck. I hoped Sarah could help me, but the words stuck on my tongue.

"Something you need to say?" she murmured as she expertly slipped the cakes onto serving platters.

Once I got started, the words spilled out in a rush. I told her about Lindsey's letter and the weird image with the tunnel. It didn't make as much sense as I'd hoped, and my voice seemed to trickle out at the end. "I think I'm seeing a possibility, but I don't know what it means."

Sarah drizzled chocolate glaze over the cakes. "Aunt Winnie will help when she gets back."

"She's not here?"

"She left with Mr. Parker this afternoon on *business*." She looked me in the eye and gave me a slow nod so I'd know what she meant.

"Dr. Card?" My throat tightened on the name so that it came out in a whisper. Last summer we stopped him from stealing a time machine, and the authorities planned to arrest him right away.

"Mr. Parker is helping now," she said. "They'll catch him soon."

The realization that he was still free sent my pulse racing. If Dr. Card was out there, something bad was going to happen, which meant I needed Aunt Winnie's help more than ever.

≪⌒≫

CHAPTER FOUR

≪⌒≫

The camp bugle woke us at sunrise the next morning, which seemed to come earlier at Camp Hawthorne than at home. I moaned and dived back onto my pillow, but Ellen poked everyone until we were awake. Her face looked pinched and white in the pale sunlight.

"Didn't you sleep last night?" I asked her.

"My braces were bothering me," she said.

"Still hurting?"

"No. They were buzzing like a radio. I kept hearing weird words like *blossomed the lovely stars.*"

"Strange."

"More than strange when it keeps you up at night," she said.

The camp bugle sounded again, and we hurried to stuff our clothes in backpacks for the camping trip. Ellen seemed impatient to get to breakfast, and I had to run to catch up with her on the trail.

"I was thinking about your braces buzzing last night. Do you think it's a new gift?" I asked.

"More like a curse—I can't control it the way I controlled my dowsing powers."

"Is it still happening?"

"No, it stopped around midnight."

"You definitely need to ask Mr. Parker about it," I said.

"Yeah, or get the stupid things removed."

Ellen cheered up while we ate Sarah's delicious buckwheat pancakes—light and buttery with a nutty flavor. Ellen dodged into the kitchen before we left, and I noticed her backpack seemed a lot bulkier when she returned.

After breakfast we hiked out to the campsite, while the ferns along the trail were wet with dew and the rising sun slanted through the trees. The woods still held the morning coolness, and we seemed to be walking under the green canopy of a different world.

The new campers started finding their gifts almost immediately. We'd barely reached the top of our first hill when word travelled down the line that a girl in the Whits had "seen" a nest in a hollow log while she was still far away.

"Another dowser," Ellen said, gritting her teeth. "Wish it was me again."

We walked in cohorts (as Niner called them) according to our dorms, with Niner in the lead and Skeeter in the back with us. The campers carried their own clothes and sleeping bags, and the telekinetics like Jayden and Joanne floated the camping gear, food and tents at the front of each cohort.

After the first hour, Niner walked up and down the line making sure everyone was okay. He complimented our dorm on the regulation backpacks we carried, and I hoped our first bad impression had blown away.

He moved on to the next group, and Ellen beckoned me to come in close. She unzipped her backpack to show me a huge box of chocolate cake mix she had smuggled inside. "Industrial-size," she said. "Won't they be surprised when I make this tonight?"

"How are you going to do it?"

"Wait and see," she said with a mysterious smile, her braces glittering in the sunlight.

I was glad Niner hadn't caught sight of the smuggled cake mix, but then I wondered why it should be a big deal anyway. Did Niner really care about little things like that?

Skeeter taught our group a trail song, and to my surprise, TJ already knew it.

"My family's passed it down for generations," TJ explained. "From a patriot who fought in the Revolutionary War."

For someone so small, she had a big voice—strong and clear—and Skeeter shushed everyone so we could hear her sing. It was a simple song about a soldier taking leave of his true-love, and the line kept repeating: "Listen, listen, listen for me."

When TJ sang, her cheeks flushed, and her stubby brown braids twitched with the music. I hoped she was getting over her homesickness. Perhaps the tune was a little bit of home she brought with her.

Soon the song spread to the Whits in front and the Twains beyond them until the words were echoing from one end of our hiking line to the other.

"See how easy it is to start something?" Skeeter said. "We've been singing this song for generations at camp."

Something fluttered in my chest. I loved the nearness I felt to my parents when I did something they had done here. *Listen, listen, listen for me.* I felt if I listened hard enough I might catch their voices in the woods, travelling across time.

With all the singing and friendly chatter, we covered a good piece of trail and arrived at our primitive campsite just before noon.

"Campers, ho," Niner called. "Sit by cohorts for your picnic lunch."

We scurried forward to claim a patch of dirt. The sun was hot now, and I swatted away the gnats that swarmed around my sweaty face. Ivan opened his water bottle and trickled a bit on his head, but I was too thirsty to waste a drop.

I was in dire need of energy. Fortunately Sarah had packed a remarkable meal—cucumber and cream cheese sandwiches, carrot sticks, strawberries, and banana cupcakes sprinkled with powdered sugar for dessert.

It was the best part of the entire primitive camp-out because after lunch it was nothing but work for the rest of the afternoon. Niner laid out the camp site in rows, with boys on one side of the clearing, girls on the other. We had to dig our own latrines, hang our food from trees to discourage bears, and put up our tents. The boys dubbed their living quarters "Fort Niner."

"Get it?" Ivan asked me. "Niner loves this stuff, and now he has a fort named after him."

The girls didn't bother naming their bedraggled collection of tents, though TJ suggested "Paradise Camp." Ellen shot that one down.

By late afternoon, I was exhausted, and I flopped on my sleeping bag for a nap. But Ellen bustled around, pulling out eggs, oil and baking mix.

She prodded me with her toe. "Come on, Stella. You have to help me make the *you-know-what.*"

I groaned and pushed myself up on one arm. "Why me?"

"Because we're a team."

It turned out her plan was to mix the cake in a pot, slap on the lid, and bury it in the white ash at the fringes of the fire. It might have worked if the ash had stayed hot, but somehow over the course of two hours, it cooled. Ellen brought out the cake in triumph only to discover it was more like pudding than cake. She clenched her teeth and moved to throw it out, but I took it away from her. "This is what your team does for you," I said.

I ladled it onto plates, and the cries of rapture over the chocolate mess attracted Joanne.

"Where'd this come from?" she demanded. "If it's contraband I have to report it to Niner."

"You wouldn't do that," I said, looking her square in the eyes. "He'd take demerits from Hawthorne House." If there was one thing I could count on, it was Joanne's insane need to win.

"I won't report you if you give me a scoop," she countered.

"Fine." I slopped a spoonful on her plate so that a splash of chocolate hit her T-shirt, but she didn't seem to notice. I left her smiling over the pudding, her eyes closed with delight.

The jubilant response finally convinced Ellen to stop grumbling.

"Is it really ok?" she asked me.

I had some of the last scrapings from the burned part at the bottom of the pot. "Chocolate tastes best with a tinge of camp fire," I told her.

"Thanks," she said quietly. "If I don't find another gift soon, I'm going to explode."

After dinner Niner called everyone together for a fire circle and announced that six kids found their gifts the first day. One of the newbies had wandered away from the group and discovered her gift for thought transference when she "heard" the telepaths calling in her mind. Another new kid realized he could understand the raccoons, who were plotting to steal our food after we went to bed.

We closed the day with an energetic sing-along, and the boys started burping along with the tunes.

"They're so disgusting," Ellen said. "I'm glad we're sleeping on the opposite side of the fire circle."

Our tent slept three if we squeezed in tight. Ellen, TJ and I laid our sleeping bags in a row. It was too hot to sleep in them, but they were useful padding and marked the boundaries for each bed.

Lying in the dark, I listened to the pulsing chirps of the crickets and gazed through the tent flap at the stars clustered above us. As soon as she got back, I'd get Aunt Winnie to teach me how to use my gift without the plague of nightmares. The thought cheered me up like Grandma's ginger cookies at Christmas. I'd help people the way my parents did, and all of Lindsey's problems would be solved. Under the sparkling canopy of stars, it didn't seem hard to believe that this summer at camp was going to be phenomenal.

"Stella, you awake?"

"Barely."

"My braces are buzzing again."

"Maybe you need a distraction…" I began sleepily.

TJ popped up and clicked on her flashlight, holding it under her chin so that she looked like a floating head. "Great idea! We need some pranks."

"Pranks?"

"Yeah, all the camp books I've ever read have pranks that the girls spring on the boys, or one team against another."

Ellen sat up, clutching her jaw. "They had that at another camp I went to. We got extra points for creativity."

I wasn't sure this was a good idea, but TJ was already crawling through the tent flap. "Let's get the guys."

We had to walk all the way across the clearing to Fort Niner. I wished I had the gift for seeing by moonlight, because I kept tripping over branches and rocks.

"Their tents are standing up much better than ours," TJ muttered as we got closer.

Just then an owl hooted, and we jumped.

I had a bad feeling about this, but my gift for seeing possibilities refused to kick in. "We should go back," I began but was interrupted by Ivan sticking his head out of a tent.

"What are you doing here?" He spoke low, but his voice squeaked on the last word.

"This is a council of war," Ellen hissed dramatically. "Get the others."

Ivan scampered out of the tent with Roy in tow. Jayden crawled out more warily.

"Hurry," Ellen said. "Before Niner wakes up."

She led the group to the fire circle where the logs still glowed red, giving a bloody atmosphere to our conference.

"We called you together to plan a prank," she announced. "TJ will explain."

TJ clapped her hand to her mouth and looked at me with wild eyes. "I can't do it," she gasped. "You t-t-tell them."

I sighed. I didn't even like this idea, but I couldn't leave TJ stammering there. "We had an idea that we could play a fun prank on one of the other teams and maybe earn some extra points."

"Cool," Ivan said.

Jayden looked at me like I'd grown two extra ears. "Are you crazy? It's more likely to *cost* us points."

Ivan and Roy gave each other a high five. "We've got the perfect plan," Ivan said. He pulled out a can of shaving cream from his backpack. "A little inspiration from my childhood with Uncle George. We spray this on the zipper of the other tents so the first person who opens the flap gets a handful of goo."

Roy chortled over the idea, and the girls cooed with admiration. "Who should we spray first?" asked TJ, happy to talk now that someone had a plan.

"How about the Fellows?" Ivan said. "They think they're better than the Thornes because their house is bigger and has its own lawn."

We made our way back to Fort Niner, with whispers and stifled giggles setting off more hooting from the owl. I was amazed no one woke up and challenged us.

Ivan found the Fellows' tents, which were set in a row with a small American flag extending from each pole. He slipped silently to the first one and unzipped the flap a few inches to insert the shaving cream can. I heard the hiss of the spray and smelled the spicy aftershave, and then suddenly a dozen flashlights snapped on in our faces.

I jumped back from the light, straining to see through the spots dancing in front of my eyes. We were surrounded by the Fellows! They must have known we were coming and set an ambush.

"Gotcha," shouted one of the kids. They cheered and whooped, and that brought Niner out of his tent.

"What's going on?" he shouted over the racket.

"We caught the perpetrators of a midnight raid," said the gotcha kid. "The owl tipped us off, sir."

Niner's flashlight swept our faces. "The Thornes, eh? Always up to trouble. That's twenty demerits and community service when we get back to camp."

"But we were just having fun," Ellen said

"No excuses," he roared. "Everyone back to bed."

I couldn't look Jayden in the eye after that. I should've done more to stop the prank, but it was too late now. My stomach churned like I was back on the bus hurtling through the tunnel, and the back of my tongue tasted bitter. I wondered if this was what guilt tasted like.

Ivan and Roy didn't seem bothered at all. They exchanged another high five and jogged back to their tent. The girls made the long walk across the clearing while the Fellows followed us with their flashlights and hooted. "Stay where you belong," and "You can't catch a Fellow napping!"

"Maybe Niner isn't serious about community service," Ellen said, but it didn't take a talent for knowing possibilities to predict we were in for trouble.

وجوب

CHAPTER FIVE

وجوب

We broke camp as the sun rose over the tips of the pine trees and the birds were beginning to sing. I didn't mind the early hour because I was eager to get back to Camp Hawthorne and see Aunt Winnie.

Our group was the last in line on the long hike back and the last to drop off our camping gear at the storage shed. I rubbed my shoulder where my backpack had rubbed a raw patch. "Home at last."

"I'm looking forward to a long afternoon nap," Ellen said.

TJ had already collapsed on the heap of sleeping bags. "I could sleep right here."

Niner strode up, his eyes glinting with purpose. "Community service today," he announced.

"But I need to see Aunt Winnie," I said.

He stared me down. "Not possible. She hasn't returned with Mr. Parker yet."

I opened my mouth to ask a question, but he cut me off. "Longfellow House is getting a new roof, and your group will clear the attic. Report for duty at thirteen hundred hours." He turned crisply and stalked away.

"Does he always talk like that?" Ellen asked.

"It's military time," TJ piped up. "I have a brother who talks that way. He says it's more precise to count the hours from zero to twenty-four hundred."

"So thirteen hundred is one o'clock?" I asked. Lindsey would probably like that—she loved crazy ways of doing things.

Ellen grumbled all the way to Longfellow House about being sentenced to hard labor.

"You forget that Jayden can move things," I said.

"He told me he won't use his powers for this."

I groaned. That meant Jayden was still mad. Working off our community service was not going to be fun.

TJ skipped along beside me, her energy already restored. "It might not be so bad. Don't you want to see what Longfellow House is like on the inside?"

"Yeah." Ellen's eyes narrowed. "Last year we only got on their porch for the card party. Do you think they're trying to hide something?"

The gotcha boy greeted us at the door, wearing a huge smirk. "Here for detention?" he asked.

"It's community service," I said, trying to look more positive than I felt. "We like helping people."

An older girl brushed past him. Her honey-blonde hair was tied up with a bandana, and she held a feather duster thick with cobwebs. "Don't mind Tad," she said, handing off the duster to him. "He was just going to finish the chandelier."

Tad slunk away, and the girl waved us through the door. "We're glad for your help. With all the dusting and polishing this place requires, we couldn't do it all ourselves."

Longfellow House was much fancier than our dorm. There were pictures on every wall and even statues and china on carved wooden bureaus. Two younger kids were polishing the banisters, and another team was dusting the room off the hall.

"Do you always work like this?" Ellen asked.

The girl shrugged. "This place and everything in it is a replica of the original house, and it's become a national historic site. Even in Longfellow's day it was famous as George Washington's headquarters during the Revolutionary War. See—Longfellow put a bust of the general at the foot of the stairs."

"He must've loved history," TJ said, peering at a framed certificate from a Native American tribe.

"He did, and he wrote lots of historical poems. Have you read any?"

I could answer that one. Thanks to Lindsey and her Longfellow phase, I'd listened to one of her favorite poems.

"*The Courtship of Miles Standish*," I said. "I liked how Priscilla told John Alden to speak for himself."

"She's my namesake—Priscilla Alden," the girl replied. "I'm the CIT here, and everyone calls me Allie. Come on—I'll give you the tour on the way to the attic."

She led us to the first room, which was even fancier than the hallway, with plush carpet and matching curtains. "Longfellow was descended from Priscilla and John Alden," she said. "That's why he wanted to tell the old stories." She stopped in front of a wall covered with portraits. "Recognize anyone?"

"Whoa—is that Nathaniel Hawthorne?" I said.

"Yes. They were friends, and Longfellow commissioned his portrait."

A delicious shiver tickled my arms. I imagined the two men planning Camp Hawthorne. I wondered if Longfellow believed in psychic phenomenon when his friend told him about it. Or was he skeptical?

The next room had a huge desk in the middle and books lining all the walls. I hoped Jayden had gotten a tour—he would love this room.

We circled back to the steps, and Allie motioned to a tall grandfather clock on the landing halfway up the stairs. "Longfellow wrote about this clock in one of his poems."

The clock gently chimed, and for a moment I felt as though I was back in Longfellow's time, when his friend Hawthorne would stop by to visit. I needed to read more of his poems, especially the one with the clock.

"I'll take you to the boys now," Allie said, leading us up the winding stairs.

I followed at the end of the line. The higher we went, the lower my stomach dropped. I didn't want to face Jayden. He'd warned us we might get in trouble, but we didn't listen. He was right to be mad at us.

But when we arrived at the top floor, the guys were laughing and talking in a wide room filled with old trunks and rickety furniture. Ivan was organizing the piles while Jayden and Roy brought more boxes from an attic door.

"This is the best community service I ever did," Jayden said, his dark face smudged with white dust. "Look at this." He held up a small wooden box, slanted on top.

"That's a portable desk," Allie said. "It belonged to George Washington."

"A reproduction, right?" Ellen said.

"There's a rumor that they sent the original items from Longfellow's house here when it became a national historic site."

"You mean this is real?" Jayden put down the desk as carefully as if it was the last dodo egg.

"Look, it opens on a hinge." Ellen lifted the lid. "And there's a scrap of paper." She held it in her palm so we could read the writing: *–nd Mine, 355,* written in faded ink.

Allie clapped her hands, clearly delighted. "I'll take this to Niner," she said. "It could be an important artifact."

After she left, we brought out the rest of the things until the attic was almost empty. It was a long, sloping space, smelling of old leather and moth balls. Soft sunshine filtered through a small window at the far end, lighting the motes of dust that swirled in the air.

At the very back lay a huge trunk, marked with a tag reading: *"This trunk was given to General Washington by Paul Revere."*

"I'll bring it out so we can see it better," Jayden said. He levitated it with a swoop of his hand and sent it floating out the attic door.

"I thought you weren't going to use your powers to help," I teased.

He shrugged. "I changed my mind about community service." He set down the trunk, and we gathered around. It was made of solid wood and bound with strips of some dull metal. From the gashes and dents in its side, it must have travelled far in its time.

"Too bad it's locked," I said, glancing at Jayden.

He stared intently at the lock, and a tiny snap told us he'd opened it.

I held my breath as he raised the lid, but there was nothing inside, except the metal lining, which still shone silver.

"I bet anything valuable was taken out long ago," Ellen said.

The guys spread tarps over the pile in the middle of the room, while TJ and I went back into the attic to sweep.

"Did you see this?" she asked. She brushed her hand over the floor, wiping away the grime. A geometric pattern had been burned into the wood. "Isn't it pretty?"

I traced the lines with my finger. It looked like diamonds arranged in a grid, with two smaller ones between each large one. Lines connected the small diamonds to form a square with an X in the middle.

The pattern flickered in front of my eyes, and I gasped. When I blinked, it came back into focus. Was there something important here? I closed my eyes as Aunt Winnie had taught me, but no further images appeared.

"Did you see something?" TJ asked, her face pale in the dim light.

"No, but there's definitely a possibility here."

TJ told the others I'd seen a possibility, and they crowded into the attic to look at the pattern in the floor.

"Maybe it's a quilt pattern," Ellen said.

"Or the map for a garden," Jayden added. "And those lines are walkways."

"But why a quilt or a garden?" I asked. "Possibilities are supposed to show something important in the future."

I'd only had one clear vision in my whole life—the time my parents travelled through time to save me from Dr. Card. My dad saw possibilities, too, and for one golden moment our gifts worked together and we thwarted Dr. Card. But our successful mission meant my parents returned to their time, and I never saw them again.

The familiar sadness swelled in my chest. My parents gave their lives to follow the "right" possibility. It didn't seem fair that the right path for their work had been exactly the wrong path for me. Their death left a gaping hole in my life. In an odd way, connecting with them last summer had only made the ache worse.

↝↜

CHAPTER SIX

↝↜

After community service, we joined the rest of the campers at the lake. We had completely missed swim certification, but Skeeter tested our group on the side. Everyone passed, even me, which proved that it's possible to remember something from one summer to the next. Now if I could only harness my gift of possibilities better.

TJ and I waded in the shallows, the sun hot on our shoulders, and then sank down into the glorious chill of the water. I hovered with my ears below the surface so that the shouts of kids grew faint. When I bobbed up, the blast of sound hit me like a wave.

Ellen splashed over to us with three swim noodles. "Let's go deeper," she said. We draped our arms over the noodles and drifted out, low waves lapping around us and the sparkle on the lake turning the water gold.

"I like it here," TJ said.

Ivan and Roy were jumping from a huge float at the far end of the swim area, and they waved to get our attention. After every cannonball jump, Ivan bobbed up and raised both hands to the sky, lighting all ten fingers and whooping. Roy copied him, yelling so loud it more than made up for the lack of fire.

But after the next round of jumps, Roy came up with his face turning purple. He thrashed and spluttered in the water as though fighting an invisible enemy.

Ivan threw an arm around him and towed him to shore, and we swam out to help. He was only half way when Roy suddenly relaxed.

"You okay?" TJ called, swimming like mad to reach him. She might have been small, but she churned through the water like a motor boat.

Roy wiped the water from his eyes and took some deep breaths. "I'm fine."

"What happened?"

He swiveled back and forth. "They were here a minute ago. Didn't you see them?"

Skeeter had joined us from the life guard stand. She put a hand on his shoulder. "You had a vision," she said.

"But it felt real—three big guys were trying to duck me underwater, and I heard them laughing."

"You've found your gift," Skeeter explained. "You can see and feel impressions from the past, probably connected to a certain place. You must have picked up a strong impression created here once."

Roy rubbed his neck, his face clouding with worry. "I was hoping for a cool gift like Ivan's."

"Mr. Parker will talk with you when he gets back," she said. "But it's not always scary like that. You'll study with the empaths, and they can help you."

Roy began shivering. We got him out of the water and found his glasses, then wrapped him in extra towels and took him up to the dining hall for hot chocolate.

Sarah fussed over him in the kitchen. "You sit down right now and eat some apple pie. That will fix those shivers."

We got pie as well—still warm from the oven with a flaky crust and cinnamon apples inside. I would have enjoyed it more if Roy didn't look so scared.

"What's with the gloomy faces?" Sarah said. "We should be celebrating. Roy's got a wonderful gift. How do you think they found King Tut's tomb or that gold ship in Florida?"

By the time Sarah finished with him, Roy was smiling again. He had three pieces of pie and two cups of hot chocolate.

"You're going to do something great—I can just feel it," Sarah declared.

After the camp fire that night, the CITs had a meeting, and the girls in our dorm stayed up late. Joanne, as the oldest, was in charge. She set up with her crew at one end, blasting some awful music from speakers. At our end, we braided each other's hair and snacked on the food we'd brought to camp. Grandma packed cherry licorice for me, and TJ had sunflower seeds.

"Sunflower seeds? What kind of snack is that?" Ellen said as she whipped out her own contribution—a huge box of chocolates.

"These are mystery chocolates," she declared. "No looking at the lid."

TJ giggled. "Is this a dare?"

"Sure, I dare you to try one."

TJ plucked a dark chocolate from the middle. "Mmm, peanut butter cream."

"I've been meaning to ask you," Ellen said. "What does TJ stand for?"

The look of bliss on TJ's face melted away. "I'd rather not say," she mumbled.

I popped a milk chocolate in my mouth. "If we went by initials, I'd be SM," I said. "For Stella Marie."

Ellen scowled. "I'd be EG for Ellen Gertrude. I hate my middle name."

"We could call you Gertie," I said with a laugh.

Ellen threw a pillow at me, and an all-out pillow fight followed until Joanne snapped off the music and told everyone to go to sleep. "Kids," she grumbled.

In the dark I heard the bunk squeak as Ellen sat up on the mattress above me. "Stella," she whispered, "the strange lines are coming again."

"What do they say?"

She took in a ragged breath. *"Where all parting, pain, and care... and death and time shall disappear."*

"Don't worry. I'm sure there's a logical explanation."

"I hope so," she replied, but for a long time I heard her turning restlessly on her cot.

I didn't sleep either. I was missing Lindsey, who had a simple way of bringing peace wherever she went. It was a relief to think she would be here soon.

≪シ✷

CHAPTER SEVEN

≪シ✷

TJ cornered me at breakfast the next morning. "Do you think there's anything wrong with me?" she asked. "It's the fourth day, and I haven't found my gift yet."

I laughed. "Last year it took me a week and a visit to the lab of a crazy scientist."

Her eyes grew wide. "That's not normal is it? The crazy scientist, I mean."

I sincerely hoped not. Aunt Winnie and Mr. Parker were supposed to be helping catch Dr. Card now, but the fact that they weren't back made me jumpy.

TJ left for swimming, and I debated whether to go or not. Aunt Winnie wasn't here for my class, but I wasn't a big fan of swimming until the sun grew hotter. While I lingered in the dining hall, Allie swished by in a colonial dress. Her honey blonde hair was stuffed under a frilly white cap so that only the bangs showed. "I'm substituting for Mr. Parker's class on thought transference. Like to join us?"

"Why are you dressed up?" I asked.

"It's my Priscilla Alden costume," she said, rubbing her hands on her skirt. "It gives me confidence when I speak in front of people."

I thought of her enthusiasm over Longfellow House and all its lore. "You'll be fine," I said.

She straightened her cap with an air of determination. "I did some research after we found the paper in George Washington's desk, and I'm using it for the class."

I joined the others in the Twain library and sat in the front row to support Allie, but she didn't need my help. As soon as she started talking, her nervousness disappeared. Her brown eyes glowed, and she paced around the room adding emphasis to her words with sweeps of her hand.

"People with ESP have done great service as spies during various wars," she began. "Especially the Revolutionary War, before the advantages of modern technology."

I sat up straighter. Was she saying that our slip of paper was from a spy?

"Some of the greatest spies were ESP practitioners. They went disguised as peddlers, farmers and smugglers, and they used codes, ciphers and invisible ink—printed between the lines of letters or in the margins of books. Not only did they find important information for General Washington, but they duped the British with false documents."

Allie paused and looked at the class. "One of the greatest of these spies was a woman with the same gift you have. She could transfer thought, and she went by the code name 355."

Code name 355? Was that the meaning of the scrap of paper? A prickle of excitement zipped down my arms, and I raised my hand. "Can you tell us more about the spies who used ESP?"

Allie smiled, clearly pleased. "Paul Revere was one of them. He used his ability for thought transference to get information and pass it to the military. He had contacts from Boston to New York. As a silversmith, he made silver bullet-shaped containers for the spies so they could hide messages. They swallowed them if they were caught. He also designed buttons used to hide documents. They placed a folded message on the button and covered it with fabric, then sewed it onto clothing."

Allie clapped her hands. "That's enough history for one day. Let's practice with thoughts, shall we?"

Though I wasn't clairvoyant, I'd been best friends with Lindsey for so long that I had plenty of practice transferring thoughts back and forth. Lindsey used to say we'd been doing it even before she discovered her gift. I really missed her.

Allie had us play *Telephone*. It worked like the regular game, except that everyone transferred thought instead of whispering messages. I could receive a thought from a clairvoyant, and the next person could transfer it from my brain. Usually I studied alone with Aunt Winnie, so it was fun to be part of a group, almost as nice as one of Sarah's hugs.

"You've got solid skills as a conduit for thought transference," Allie told me at the end of class. "Most people block it as a reflex, but you know how to stay open. You ought to develop it more."

After lunch we had an activity on the lake. I was one of the first to arrive, and I sat on the shore, looking out at the pine trees ringing the water under the blue sky. I always felt close to my parents when I sat here, perhaps because it was the first image I ever had of Camp Hawthorne when I found it online. At the end of camp last year, I'd sat in this same spot to read a letter from my parents—the only one I'd ever had. They told me they loved me and were proud of me, but their words left me with a vague feeling that their work wasn't done, even though they were gone.

The campers filtered onto the beach, and Eugene in his black CIT shirt called the Thornes into a huddle. "Today is a relay race with canoes, and this is our chance to shine," he said, shaking his spiked head like an angry hawk. "The Whits are leading by thirty points, but we can overtake them."

"Thornes!" Ivan yelled, lighting his fingers.

"Thornes!" Roy echoed. He was looking better after the episode on the lake yesterday.

Joanne was there too, looking tough with a sweatband around her forehead and her long black hair streaming behind her in the wind. For once I was glad she was on my team.

Eugene divided us into groups, with strong paddlers distributed evenly. TJ and I were with Jayden, which meant we were the weak paddlers.

"Niner says to keep your eye on the goal," Jayden told us as he handed us our life jackets.

It seemed a shame to waste canoeing on races. Ever since I'd discovered the delight of splashing paddles and glinting sunlight, I liked to take it slow. I sighed and turned to the canoes waiting on the shore.

The event was a relay race to the weedy island in the center of the lake and back again. Every canoe had a number, and the crew had to beach the canoe, find the numbered message for their craft, and bring it back. The messages were mounted on sticks sunk in the sand, so they weren't supposed to be hard to find, but the relay turned into a chaos of kids yelling and canoes bumping into each other. When each team returned, they passed the canoe to the next group and ran to Niner to read their message. The beach was a tangle of kids handing off paddles, wobbling into canoes and shouting at each other.

The Fellows, as always, had their own paddling chant, which pushed them forward across the water:

> By the shores of Gitche Gumee,
> By the shining Big-Sea-Water...

The first Thorne group with Ivan, Roy and Ellen kept up with them, partly due to Ellen's willpower and bossiness, though Ivan's long arms might have helped.

The second crew was led by Joanne, and I had to admit she was good. She scooped the paddle through the water and shouted "faster" so ferociously that her teammates paddled at double-speed. By the time the fourth squad reached the island for their round, we were in second place. Ellen yelled until her face was as red as her hair.

"Our group is next," I said, pulling TJ into place. Jayden leaned forward like a sprinter ready to take off, and TJ in her orange life vest bounced and cheered. I flexed my fingers on the paddle, hoping we could hold our place for the final round. Ellen would never forgive me if we didn't.

Joanne strode up and grabbed TJ's paddle. "I'll take this."

"Wait a minute—we're next," I said.

"I know." Joanne's voice was flat, and her gaze flicked over me as though I were a bug not worth stepping on. "She's too little. We'll lose if I don't help."

"That's cheating," I said.

She shrugged. "What if it is?"

I grabbed the paddle back, surprised at my own courage, and pressed it into TJ's hands.

"Thornes are not cheaters," I said.

"Let's go!" roared Jayden.

TJ jumped in the canoe, as though propelled by a girl-sized catapult, and Jayden and I pushed the canoe off the beach and hopped in.

I caught a last glimpse of Joanne glowering at us.

"Thornes! Thornes!" the others yelled, and we took off across the water. Jayden bent over his paddle, and TJ and I strained to keep up with him. My anger at Joanne gave my arms power, and I kept my eyes fixed on the island.

"Almost there," Jayden called. "Get ready to find our message."

"The message," TJ chirped. "I see it—It says *the race is not to the swift.*"

Whoa—TJ saw it before we even got there. That meant...

Our canoe bumped up onto the beach. "Go get it, TJ," I yelled. She was so intent on the relay, she didn't realize she'd found her gift.

Jayden and I turned the canoe "TJ can read hidden writing," I crowed, and we knocked paddles in our version of a high five.

TJ scampered back toward the boat, her face beaming. Her quick retrieval gave us an edge, and my arms pumped with new energy as we paddled back toward shore. But even as we raced back, the murmuring chant of the Fellows churned behind, growing louder by the second.

"Faster," Ellen yelled. We were so close I could see the sun shining on her braces. TJ didn't wait for us to land. She launched herself onto the beach and sprinted to Niner with our final message. The Fellows' runner was right behind her, but she got to Niner first. The Thornes whooped and cheered.

I sat back in the canoe, waving and smiling at TJ as the Thornes lifted her to their shoulders for her victory march. She grinned back at me, her eyes wide with wonder.

"You did it, TJ—you found your gift," I shouted.

"Thornes," yelled Ivan, lighting all ten fingers.

Joanne had conveniently disappeared.

❧❧

CHAPTER EIGHT

❧❧

The next morning we had cinnamon rolls and scrambled eggs for breakfast. TJ and I arrived early, and I volunteered to be the runner for our table. I liked the job because the wall next to the kitchen was covered with rows of canoe paddles, recording the head counselors through the years. Every time I passed, I'd find my parents' names near the top of a middle row. It was like tagging home or seeing a familiar face.

Pausing with the full tray, I stared at their names and breathed in the cinnamon rising from the steaming rolls. I sighed happily and turned toward my table. TJ waved at me with her fork, and I held up the tray to show off the rolls. But before I could take the first step, someone pushed me from behind. The plates flew off the tray, and I fell, pain crashing through my knees. I jumped up to demand an explanation and saw Joanne disappear through the swinging door to the kitchen, her long black hair flicking behind her.

TJ rushed to my aid. "You okay?" It looked like the start of tears in her eyes, so I swallowed my groans and dusted myself off.

"Nothing a new batch of cinnamon rolls won't help."

"I'll get them!" She scooped the jumble of food onto the tray and took off at a run. She paused at the kitchen door to free one hand for pushing it open, but the door swung toward her and she jumped. The tray flew through the air and hit Joanne in the face.

Joanne screamed, long and piercing. Eggs clung to her hair and face, and the syrupy cinnamon rolls left a brown stain down the front of her white camp T-shirt. "You little freak—what do you think you're doing?"

TJ was trying to clean the floor, but Joanne yanked her up by the arm. "You did that on purpose!"

The yelling brought Niner from the kitchen. "Twenty demerits from Hawthorne House," he bellowed, and Joanne's mouth snapped shut.

Tears rolled down TJ's face, but she returned to the floor to scrape the rest of the food onto the tray.

I limped forward to help her, irritation pinching my insides. Why didn't Niner see what was going on?

Joanne had him by the elbow and was talking fast and low. We stood up to take the heap of eggs and rolls to the kitchen, but Niner planted himself in front of us. "Joanne told me what happened, and I'm adding community service for you two."

"What about Joanne?" I said, but Niner held up a hand.

"Arguing is not going to reduce your punishment," he replied with a smug smile.

Unbelievable! Niner wouldn't even listen to our side of the story.

"You're wrong—" began TJ, but I pulled her into the kitchen before we made things worse.

Ellen was already there, wearing an apron and frowning at a pan she was stirring on the stove. "Don't interrupt me," she muttered. "I've got to get this right."

Sarah took one look at TJ's face, still red from crying, and came around the cook table to give her a hug. "What's wrong? Still homesick?"

TJ rubbed her eyes. "No, it's Joanne. She's picking on us, and Niner thinks it's our fault."

"The right will come out in the end," Sarah said. "You've got to turn your mind to other things." She rummaged in the oversized pocket of her cook's apron and pulled out a slim blue volume. "Look, I found that book of Mr. Longfellow's poetry you were asking about."

TJ took it eagerly.

"See if the poem about the clock is in there," I said.

TJ gave a little jump when she found it. "This is the one Allie told us about." She read it aloud on the spot. It was about a clock that witnessed everything in a house—births, weddings and funerals. The end was sad because everyone from the house was gone.

TJ read the last lines:

Never here, forever there,
Where all parting, pain, and care,
And death, and time shall disappear, —
Forever there, but never here!

The lines sounded familiar, but I couldn't remember where I'd heard them before.

"Oh no!" Ellen brandished a spoon at the pan, which had erupted in flames. Sarah darted to her side and clapped on the lid, and the fire disappeared.

Ellen slumped. "Cooking is definitely not my gift."

"Lots of other gifts out there," Sarah said, guiding her to a chair by the cook table. "You three eat some eggs and cinnamon rolls, and see how things look after that."

While we ate, Sarah asked us for more details on Joanne.

"She just doesn't like us, and we don't know why," I said.

Sarah was scrubbing the blackened pan from the fire, and she paused. "Have you tried forgiving her?"

"She never said she was sorry."

"Hmm, sometimes forgiveness has to come first."

I had no idea what Sarah meant. There had to be some way to get back at Joanne and make her stop picking on us.

After breakfast Sarah asked Niner if we could do our community service in the kitchen. Ellen stayed, too. We chopped apples and chicken for a salad, and she taught us how to whip meringue for lemon pies. "Even if you don't have a gift for cooking you can learn the skills," she said.

"How long did it take you to develop your gift?" I asked.

She stopped with a spoonful of meringue in mid air and laughed her hearty laugh. "I've been learning my whole life, honey. You never stop learning."

∂∽

Ivan was in rare form at lunch. "The way I figure it, we've been at camp for five days," he said. "And we haven't done anything spectacular yet."

TJ was making a peanut butter and pickle sandwich, and she giggled. "Maybe we should have a secret mission to do something spectacular."

I wondered what Niner would think about Ivan's idea of spectacular, but then I decided I didn't care. He would never be fair with us anyway. We might as well go for as much fun as we could.

"If this is a mission, we need code names," Ellen said.

"How about our middle names?" I asked.

Ellen made a face. "That means I'll be Gertrude, and you'll be Marie."

"And I'll be Joseph," Ivan said.

We looked at TJ.

"I'll be J," she said, taking a huge bite out of her sandwich.

Ivan leaned over his plate and whispered urgently: "Agent Joseph to Agent Gertie—permission granted to initiate something spectacular with fire?"

Ellen pretended to be busy adding lettuce to her sandwich. "I will never admit to being Agent Gertie."

Ivan grinned impishly and made a motion like he was making a snowball, except orange fire glowed between his fingers. "Jayden needs a little baseball practice."

I squirmed in my seat. "He'll never agree to it."

"Agent J, then." Ivan winked.

TJ quivered with delight, her wispy braids switching around her head. "Good thing I brought my bat."

"Meet me behind the canoe shack at the free swim today. Agent Joseph signing off."

❧❧

The afternoon activity was held at Whittier House. TJ had never been there, so I showed her the way, turning down the dusty path from the Junction Stone. The Whits lived in a tidy white house with green shutters. It looked as old as ours, but more cheerful. Neatly-trimmed bushes lined the front of the house with two baskets of marigolds blooming on either side of the front steps.

It had a parlor that stretched from the front of the house to the back, and they had filled the room with rough wooden tables. A dozen campers were working on projects, and I sniffed the tangy smell of burning pine. We took a seat next to Ellen, and Skeeter gave us slices from a thick tree branch. They still had the bark on them. "You can burn anything you like into this," she said, handing each of us a wood burning tool.

She showed us the disk she had made. It had the motto "Honk if you love bikes."

"It's for my mother," she explained. "She's a bike enthusiast, even sent me a bike to use at camp."

"She *sent* a bike?" I said.

"She works for a bicycle company, and she had it shipped. It just came today, and Jayden put it together for me. You can use it anytime you want."

"Thanks." I was fascinated with the idea of riding a bike that came through the mail.

I looked around to see what the others were doing, hoping to get some inspiration.

Joanne sniggered and nudged the girl beside her. I caught a glimpse of a heart with the letters J+A on her circle of wood. If J was for Joanne, I wondered who the unlucky A would be.

Ivan didn't use the wood-burning tool. He doodled with his fingernail and had a pretty good picture of a squirrel. He also kept busy changing out the hot metal tips for anyone who was afraid to do it with pliers.

I decided to make a "Welcome" sign for Grandma to hang on the front door. Her new hobby was hosting neighborhood parties—it didn't matter the occasion. We'd had baby showers and welcome-home parties, even a birthday for a neighborhood dog. She could use the sign year-round.

Thinking about Grandma sent a lump rolling up my throat. I pictured the way her eyes crinkled when she had a surprise for me. We still read books together, taking turns to read aloud, and she'd let me stay up late if the book was really good. I wished I could tell her about the ESP part of camp. She would love the mystery and adventure.

While we worked, Allie told us about her class, which I missed thanks to Niner's community service. "I had more history for them today," she said. "Did you know that Mark Twain was working on making thought transference available to everyone? He named his idea the telectroscope, and he wrote about it in a story set in the future. He actually predicted the internet."

"So the internet does the same thing as thought transference, only you don't need a special gift?" I asked.

"Yeah." She went back to doodling with the wood burning tool.

"Doesn't it bother you that your gift is being replaced?"

"Not really. Mine works without electricity."

She had a point there.

Skeeter came around to check our work and looked over my shoulder. "Not too hard, Stella. Let the tool do the work. Too much pressure will bend the tip."

I relaxed my grip on the tool and let it glide slowly over the wood. Right away it started working better. It was funny how lots of things worked that way. Ellen, for example. She was trying so hard to get back her gift or find a replacement. If she didn't let up, the pressure might break her.

I glanced at TJ, who wore a faraway look. She had moved on from her slice of wood to doodling on the rough wood of the work bench. It was an exact replica of the pattern we found in the attic.

"What are you doing?" Ellen said, the sharp note in her voice jerking TJ out of her dream world. She looked down at the table and her eyes grew round. "I forgot I didn't have a piece of wood in front of me." She ran her hand over the surface and studied the pattern. "I wish we knew what it meant," she said.

Ellen squinted at the design. "Could it be a map?"

"That would explain why it was important," I said. "But I never saw a map like that."

At the end of craft time I started for the door, but Joanne blocked my way. "You enjoy your community service?" she said with a smirk.

"Move," I said.

"Not til you admit you're sorry for making a mess of my shirt."

"You know it wasn't my fault. You barged into TJ." I was so mad my ears were burning. I couldn't believe Sarah thought I should forgive Joanne. What ever happened to everything turning out all right?

Joanne shoved me. "Say you're sorry."

"Only if you say sorry first!" I ducked under her arm and ran as fast as I could. I looked behind me and caught Joanne's seething glare. I didn't have to use my possibilities to know she was out to get me.

༺༄༅༻

CHAPTER NINE

༺༄༅༻

After the run-in with Joanne I needed to blow off some steam. I jogged all the way to Ivan's meeting spot at the canoe shack, a weathered gray building made of warped wooden planks. He was already there, wearing his cowboy hat and lounging against the wall.

The first group of swimmers was splashing around, and more campers were arriving. Cries of "race you to the water!" and "watch out for the ball!" mixed with the slap of the waves against the float at the end of the swim area.

"A good turnout today for our little show," Ivan said, giving me a conspiratorial wink.

Still breathless from running, I nodded agreement and gulped in the soft lake breeze, which smelled of pine and honeysuckle and coconut suntan lotion.

"Is there time for a quick swim?" I asked. The cool water would feel lovely on sweaty legs and arms.

Ivan looked shocked. "Before our mission?"

I had to be content with a quick dash to the lake for a pail of water to splash over my head. On the way back I caught sight of Ellen's red hair as she picked her way down the hill to the beach. TJ skipped behind her singing a chorus of "Listen, listen." She had a bat tucked under her arm.

They arrived and Ivan's grin was so wide he might have been welcoming the President of the United States. "Let the mission begin!"

"What's your plan?" Ellen asked him.

"You have to say *Agent Gertie checking in with Agent Joseph*," Ivan whispered.

Ellen gritted her teeth, and her braces sparked in the sunlight. "You do it, Stella."

"Agent Marie to Agent Joseph," I whispered dramatically. "What's the plan?"

Ivan tapped the mound of packets beside him. "I've invented a new kind of fireworks, and this afternoon will be their premier performance."

"Why do you need the bat?" TJ asked.

"To launch them, of course. I may be able to make fire, but I can't throw them as high as we need."

TJ pulled a baseball cap from her back pocket and tugged the brim over her eyes. Then she stooped and sifted some sandy dirt through her hands and flexed her fingers around the bat. "I'm ready."

"You're up, Agent J." Ivan stepped back and got ready to pitch.

"Wait! Is this safe?" I asked.

"Of course—what could go wrong?"

I could think of a dozen things that could go wrong with fire. I squinted at the lake. Clear skies, a couple dozen kids jumping off the float and splashing around in the water, and the life guards on duty.

"First pitch," sang out Ivan. He threw a small orange packet in a slow arc, and TJ bit her lip and concentrated on the "ball."

Crack! The packet flew up in the air, and gray smoke trailed behind it. At the highest point, it burst into flames, shooting out petals of orange fire like a giant flower. The sparkles hung on the air for a moment, the memory of a fire flower, and then a gentle rain of ash fell on the water.

The kids in the lake shouted, and even the life guards clapped their hands.

Ivan wound up for another pitch, and TJ smashed it into the sky. This time the fire was blue, and it seemed to chase its tail around and around before disintegrating into tiny sparks that melted to nothing.

More swimmers were arriving, and they dashed into the water, pointing up at the sky.

Ivan pitched one firecracker after another—explosions that whistled like snakes, bursts of purple, green and red, and even a huge orange "N" that left a shadow of smoke behind. "That was for Niner," Ivan explained.

I scanned the lake—where was Niner?

"And now for the grand finale!" Ivan hoisted a packet the size of a football. "Think you can do it, Agent J?"

TJ swung the bat a few times and studied the firecracker. "I got it."

She grunted when the bat made contact, but it was a beautiful hit. The packet spiraled through the air, higher and higher. I held my breath, ready for the final light show. But instead of brilliant lights, black smoke poured from the packet and banging shots cracked over our heads, like an entire western shoot-out in a tin bucket. With every shot, the firecracker zigzagged to the side.

Ivan tore at his hair and ran toward the lake. "Everyone, out of the water!" He waved his arms and yelled, but the kids were too intent on watching the smoking firework.

It began to fall back toward the lake, and tongues of fire flew from it—orange, red and yellow. It flamed hotter and hotter, until with a final crashing boom, it exploded above our heads.

Hundreds of fiery bits of paper floated softly down on the beach, and Ivan slumped with relief. But not for long. Niner strode toward him, an entirely different version of fireworks going off in his eyes.

"Should we run?" asked TJ.

"No, this is our mission, remember?" I said. "Something spectacular."

But TJ was trembling as we crept from behind the canoe shack to stand beside Ivan.

"Who is responsible for this?" Niner roared.

Ivan stepped forward—his face set like he was facing his doom. "I am."

"Fifty demerits from the Thornes." Niner yelled so loud the veins stood out on his neck and his face was red. "You could have burned down the entire camp—harmed the campers." He refilled his lungs for more roaring, though we were only five feet away. "Community service! Pick up every bit of scrap and ash on this beach. If I find even a particle of fireworks, you will be sent home." He turned on his heel and blew his whistle. "Everyone, out of the lake!"

The other campers grumbled and frowned at us as they wrapped their towels around their shoulders and hiked up the hill to camp. I was glad Jayden wasn't here to see this. He would have been frowning with the rest.

The burned scraps were almost impossible to collect. They turned to ash when we touched them, and our hands grew slimy with sweat and soot. I felt like a smoking firecracker myself. Niner didn't get it. He couldn't see the fun in camp, and he was determined to ruin it for everyone else.

Ellen rubbed a blackened hand across her cheek. "Remind me to say 'no' to any future spectacular plans from Agent Joseph."

Ivan bounced up with a load of blackened paper stashed in his T-shirt, which he had converted to a bag. I suspect he thought Niner's yelling was all part of the game.

"I've got our next plan all mapped out," he said. "We'll impersonate a flying saucer!"

Ellen and I groaned.

৵৩৵

At dinner all the CITs were missing again and Jayden too, but tonight we discovered the reason.

Skeeter directed us to the barn at Alcott House, where a curtain had been hung on one side of the platform. Jayden was working behind it, and I jumped up on stage to greet him.

"The audience isn't allowed back here," he said.

"Where have you been all afternoon?"

"Helping Niner set up the show." His shoulders straightened, and I could tell he was proud to be asked.

"I bet you were a big help with lifting things," I said.

"Yeah," and for the first time he grinned. "Save a seat for me, okay?"

The campers filled every chair and every bit of floor in the front. I found the others sitting on the ground off to the side.

Excited chatter filled the room, and Ellen had to yell to be heard. "What's going on?"

"Jayden didn't say."

He squeezed in with us at the last minute, just as the lights went down.

A spot light blinked on and Niner, dressed in a Colonial uniform, stepped from behind the curtain. A hush fell on the crowd.

"Welcome to *The Midnight Ride of Paul Revere* by Henry Wadsworth Longfellow," he boomed.

"Longfellow?" Ellen whispered. "Isn't that Lindsey's favorite?"

I nodded, wishing she could be here.

Niner held a scroll of parchment which he proceeded to unroll. He waited for absolute silence and then began to read.

> *Listen, my children, and you shall hear*
> *Of the midnight ride of Paul Revere.*

The lines rolled on, and Eugene stalked onstage, dressed as a patriot with a blue jacket and tricorn hat covering his spiked hair. He held a lantern in his hand.

Skeeter followed him. I almost didn't recognize her without the art pencils sticking out of her bun, which was tucked under a cap. Niner continued:

> *He said to his friend, "If the British march*
> *By land or sea from the town to-night,*
> *Hang a lantern aloft in the belfry arch*
> *Of the North Church tower as a signal light,--*
> *One if by land, and two if by sea;*

Eugene handed her the lantern and mimed rowing across the stage, while a sheet painted with a magnificent sailing boat, glided from behind the curtain and took a position in the corner.

> *Where swinging wide at her moorings lay*
> *The Somerset, British man-of-war.*

The rhythm of the poem mesmerized me. Skeeter and the CITs performed the story with sound effects for the horses' hooves and the tramping of soldier feet. They even had a fog machine that filled the stage with a gauzy mist about two feet high. Allie in her colonial dress played a country woman awaking to hear the warning cry.

At the end, the farmers with their muskets chased the Redcoats down the lane, and Niner had to pause while the audience clapped and cheered.

His voice grew mellow as he recited the closing lines:

For, borne on the night-wind of the Past,
Through all our history, to the last,
In the hour of darkness and peril and need,
The people will waken and listen to hear
The hurrying hoof-beats of that steed,
And the midnight message of Paul Revere.

The barn erupted with stamping feet and shrill whistles, and the CITs came out for a bow.

I caught Jayden's eye. "Lindsey would have loved this," I said.

"Any more clues?" he asked.

I shook my head, and he frowned. If only Aunt Winnie would come back. I escaped Jayden's disapproving look and went with the others to get some bug juice and brownies at the back of the barn.

Allie, tugging at her colonial cap, found me there. "Wasn't that a wonderful play?" she asked.

TJ was stuffing her mouth with a huge brownie and nodded her agreement.

"Paul Revere is one of my favorite patriots," Allie said, her words tumbling out the way they did when she got excited. "He was a spy in Boston and did lots of things people don't even know about, like retrieving John Hancock's trunk for General Washington."

"What was so important about the trunk?" Jayden asked, joining our group.

"Valuable papers inside."

"We found a trunk in the attic after you left," TJ piped up.

"I wonder if it's the same one—did you find anything in it?"

"Nothing but the shiny silver lining," I said, and at the same moment the picture of the trunk blossomed in my mind. I closed my eyes tight and tried to get the image to go further. "Come on," I muttered, but the trunk disappeared as quickly as it had come.

Jayden must have been watching me. "A possibility?"

"No," I snapped. "Stop bothering me about it."

৵৽

CHAPTER TEN

৵৽

After refreshments Niner gathered a crowd around him. I pretended I wasn't interested and lingered near the doorway. I'd wait for the others and walk back with them.

The throng broke up, and Jayden jogged over, a sappy smile on his face. "Niner personally challenged me to join his new boot camp. He said it will make me a better athlete."

"You're already an incredible athlete," I said. I knew I should have been more encouraging, but something about Niner lit a fire in my brain.

"Telekinetics only helps so far. With boot camp I can increase my running speed and core body strength."

Ivan wandered over from the fringes of the crowd. "You're not joining, too?" I demanded.

He shrugged. "I like running."

"But you don't like waking up in the morning."

"I can run in my sleep."

৵৽

The next morning I woke up to the sound of a military chant and drumming footsteps on the path that ran by Hawthorne House.

First in place you build a chain--
Send it out and back again
Sound-off; 1 - 2; Sound-off; 3 – 4!

I groaned and squashed my pillow over my head.

Even worse, the only topic of conversation at breakfast was boot camp.

"Boot camp is going to give us better self-control," Ivan said, lighting one of his fingers and grinning at me mischievously.

"Niner says it keeps us in step and builds teamwork," Jayden added.

Ellen's face puckered. "It's almost like thought-transference. The whole line in sync—thinking one thought."

I didn't want my friends in sync with Niner. After all, he was the one who doled out community service like he was camp dictator.

Jayden must have picked up on my feelings. "Sometimes you have to start over," he said.

That was the problem. I didn't want to start over. I wanted to prove to Niner that he was wrong about me— make him take back all the injustice.

౿౿ఞ

Mr. Parker and Aunt Winnie returned at last at lunch. They were sitting at a table in the dining hall—Mr. Parker in his green bow tie and suspenders and Aunt Winnie in her wheelchair, her brown face wrinkled in a smile.

Jayden and I swooped down on them, and Ellen wasn't far behind. I knew she wanted to ask Mr. Parker about her braces.

But when we got to the table, Mr. Parker held up a hand. "I know you have a lot to tell us, but it will have to wait." He turned to a heavy-set man beside him. "This is the foreman who will direct the roofing project at Longfellow House. I understand your team was kind enough to clear the attic for the workers."

Mr. Parker gave us one of his lop-sided grins, but there was something in his eyes that was wary.

"But Mr. Parker, I've been dying to talk to you," Ellen said. "I got braces, and…"

"Wait," he said, more sternly this time. Ellen's mouth snapped shut.

"We were wondering if Lindsey came with you," I said.

Mr. Parker pulled a letter from his pocket. "I just got the news she will come tomorrow." He excused himself and made his way to the podium for announcements. Everyone clapped to welcome him back. On the outside Mr. Parker hadn't changed a bit from last year—same black high tops and green bow tie and same welcoming smile—but still, there was something different in the way he walked to the podium. He seemed tired.

"I'd like to thank Niner and Skeeter for taking care of everything while I was gone," he began. "We will have roofers on the premises for the next three days, and you must all be on your best behavior. Unless you live at

Longfellow House, stay clear of the building while the roof is repaired. Finally, new campers will have orientation activities this afternoon, and everyone else will have driving try-outs."

"What are driving try-outs?" I asked.

Ellen had grown quiet, and she pulled us away from Aunt Winnie's table. "I don't think the roofers know we're an ESP camp. We better talk over here."

As it turned out, she didn't know what driving try-outs were either. "But I'll find out," she said. "Getting information is one thing I can still do."

The answer must have been harder to find than she anticipated because she didn't return after lunch. I wheeled Aunt Winnie back to her cabin, hoping to tell her about Lindsey, but she wouldn't let me begin. She told me about her pigs and chickens and how many new ones had been born since I was at camp last year. "And the new chicks are the boldest creatures you ever saw. They walk right through the door and peck at the flowers on my quilt."

We finally arrived at her cabin, and I settled her with a cup of tea. She took one sip and put it down, her eyes alert. "Now, Stella, tell me what's bothering you."

"Were you waiting to talk until we were safe from the roofers?" I asked.

"Did your gift tell you that?"

"No, just commonsense."

I gave her Lindsey's letter, and she muttered to herself while she read it. When she finished, she sat back in her wheelchair and squinted at me. "Did you figure out what she wanted?"

"I've had some twinges but nothing made sense. The first time it was Lindsey's house going blurry. The second time, my mind flashed on a dark tunnel. The third time we were in the attic at Longfellow House and there was a pattern burned in the floor that went wavery on me."

Aunt Winnie stared at the ceiling, where the herbs and flowers hung drying. "It's a good start."

"There's something else. Ellen's getting strange sentences transmitted through her braces."

"Has she been writing them down?" Her sharp tone startled me.

"I don't know."

"Tell her to record as many as she can remember. I'll notify Mr. Parker, and he will arrange a meeting—somewhere safe."

Aunt Winnie was more demanding during our lesson than she'd ever been before. She made me bring up a picture of an old memory and hold it as long as possible, then step forward slowly, image by image, to see what happened next. I started with my seventh birthday party, and then tried my first day of sixth grade. It got easier as we went along, and by the end of class I was exhausted but pleased.

"Good progress," Aunt Winnie said. "Keep practicing on your own, and I'll see you tomorrow."

I turned to leave, but Aunt Winnie called me back. "I have something else for you," she said softly. She held an envelope in her hand, and I froze. The handwriting was a precise scientific printing. A letter from my dad.

My legs wobbled, and I sank onto Aunt Winnie's bed. It took a while to open the envelope because I didn't want to tear the flap. My dad had sealed this letter over ten years ago, before he died. I read:

Dear Stella,

We've asked Aunt Winnie to give you this letter when you return for your second year at camp. It is hard to imagine not being there to see you grow up, but I have seen the possibility and thought it best to write to you in advance.

We have to let you know, darling, that the work we do has become increasingly risky. We've turned down many missions because we want to be there for you, Stella. But there's one last job we have to do. There's a promise we made. If we don't finish, we need you to see it through.

I hope it will not be necessary for this letter to come to you, but if it does, we trust you will know what is true and right.

Love,
Daddy and Mom

I sat staring at the letter for a long time. Aunt Winnie laid a gentle hand on my arm. "Your father was confident you would know what to do at the right time. That is why our work here is so important."

A heavy weight seemed to settle in the pit of my stomach. I just hoped I could live up to my parents' expectations.

❧

Driving try-outs took place late in the afternoon. Jayden and I walked there together, and I told him about the letter and my progress with Aunt Winnie. He nodded approvingly. "If you keep working on it, you'll be able to help Lindsey when she gets here."

But I wasn't so confident. I gazed ahead through the green gloom of light under the trees.

Suddenly Niner stepped onto the path, seemingly from nowhere. His gray camp T-shirt mingled with the trunks of the trees, and it hit me—Niner's gift was camouflage! No wonder he always seemed to appear when we least expected it.

"Did you see that?" I whispered to Jayden. "We just witnessed Niner's gift. He can camouflage himself." We looked again, but Niner had disappeared.

"Cool gift," Jayden said.

"But he's using it against us. We need to defend ourselves."

Jayden shrugged. "If you don't do anything wrong, you won't have anything to worry about."

"But I haven't been doing anything wrong, and I'm still getting in trouble every day."

"You sure?"

"Ninety demerits from the Thornes—you don't think that's trouble?"

Jayden shifted his feet. "Most of those were just misunderstandings."

"That's what I'm trying to say."

I felt a heavy hand on my shoulder. "How's everything with the Thornes?" Niner said in his booming voice. I ducked away to stand next to Jayden.

"Everything good, sir," he said, raising his hand to his forehead in a stiff salute.

"I'm counting on you, Sergeant."

Niner returned the salute and walked away.

"What was that about?" I asked.

Jayden dropped his hand but kept his shoulders tall and square. "He's deputized me to help the Thornes keep the rules."

"You never worried about rules before," I said.

"Niner says it's part of growing up," he replied.

"So I'm a baby—"

"I'm not saying that. It's just we're not little kids anymore, now that we know about our gifts."

I wasn't sure I wanted to grow up. If it meant following rules and never having fun, I'd be glad to stay a kid.

The excitement over finding Niner's secret drained away. Jayden was going over to the enemy! I was about to ask him if he was crazy, when everything went wobbly. I closed my eyes like Aunt Winnie taught me and tried to focus on what I was seeing, but I was so mad at Jayden, the only image that came was the silly smirk on Niner's face when he called him "Sergeant."

Aunt Winnie would say to concentrate on the pictures, not my feelings. I tried to pull Jayden into the image—his curly black hair and broad shoulders—and suddenly the images started rolling forward like a slide show. I was doing it! But I didn't like what I saw. Picture after picture showed Jayden following Niner: the two of them in the dining hall...on the stage...at the lake... at the Junction Stone. Just when I thought I couldn't take it anymore, the images split. On the left Jayden helped Niner dig up something behind the stone. On the right, Ellen and I arrived and helped them.

"Stella, are you all right?"

I felt Jayden's hands gripping my arms. The vision disappeared, and I opened my eyes. His face was bent over me, so close I saw the pupils in his dark brown eyes. "Were you seeing possibilities?" he asked.

He looked like the old Jayden, my best friend in kindergarten. The one who helped me limp home when I wiped out on my bike. But I didn't trust him now. "I might have," I said. "But it stopped before I got anything useful."

"Keep practicing like Aunt Winnie told you," he said.

I pulled away from him. "If you had this gift, you'd know it's harder than it looks."

"That's not what I meant—"

But I stalked away, not even looking back.

⊷⊱

CHAPTER ELEVEN

⊷⊱

The driving try-outs took place in the pasture behind Whittier House. Orange cones marked off a circular track, and beyond it, a long barn stood with both doors open. Everyone who successfully steered around the track would have a turn at driving through the barn.

"I thought you had to have a license to drive," Ellen said.

"These are go-carts," Skeeter explained. "But they make a good driving test."

Ellen pulled me toward the marker where we were supposed to line up. "I need to do this," she said. "I told Mr. Parker about losing my dowsing powers, and he didn't have any solutions."

"What exactly are you trying to do?" I asked.

"Isn't it obvious? They're testing us to find campers who can transport through tunnels."

I watched Niner bring the first go-cart chugging around the track. It didn't look particularly safe, especially when he gunned it around the corners. "Those go-carts seem faster than regular ones."

Ellen smiled with satisfaction. "I'm going to do this."

Niner pulled next to us and hopped out of the cart. "Listen up, everyone. There are rules you need to know. Everyone must wear a seat belt and a safety helmet. There's a governor switch for speed, which you MUST NOT touch. Be safe and do your best to stay within the cones."

Before he even finished, Ellen crawled into the go-cart and fastened the seatbelt. She clicked the strap on the helmet and turned to give me a thumbs-up sign.

"Be safe," Niner said, as he took off the brake for her.

Ellen gripped the wheel, and the cart jumped ahead, the engine growling as it picked up speed. It swerved a little at first, but she brought it in line and turned the first corner without knocking over any cones. A straight stretch came next, and she leaned forward, pushing the go-cart faster.

"Not too fast," Niner yelled in his megaphone voice, but I don't think she heard.

She maneuvered the second corner despite the speed and seemed to slow for the third turn. But as she came down the final stretch, the engine revved and the go-cart hurtled forward. Ellen jerked back, shouting and waving her arm at the crowd at the end of the track. The look on her face was pure terror.

Niner sprang into action. He swept away the cones from the last turn.

"Clear the way!" he yelled, and everyone scooted back.

Ellen zipped by, and he jumped onto the go-cart, steering it through the open pasture until it sputtered to a stop.

The crowd of kids grew deathly quiet, and Ellen limply crept from the cart. Niner bent over the dash board, shaking his head.

Behind me Joanne and her gang started laughing.

"It's not funny," I said.

"Aw, your friend got scared?" Joanne spoke in a mock baby voice.

Jayden stared at her, and then pulled me aside. "She's hiding something."

Ellen stalked back to us while Niner drove the cart back to the starting point.

"Someone turned off the governor, and the cart went crazy," she muttered, her eyebrows drawing together. "Niner gave ten demerits to the Thornes. Wouldn't believe it wasn't me."

Joanne was craning forward, trying to hear what she said, and I suddenly knew what happened. Joanne used her telekinetic powers to sabotage that cart.

"Give me the helmet," I said. "I'm going next."

"Oooh—Stella's not afraid of a go-cart." Joanne started a slow clap that the rest of her gang picked up.

Clap—clap—clap.

I was so mad I forgot to be scared. I tightened the seatbelt, and the idling engine drowned out the clapping and jeers. *I can do this* I told myself.

"Don't raise this switch," Niner barked, and I nodded. Then he took off the brake, and I chugged slowly forward. I pressed the accelerator lightly, and it was easy to control the speed. I put-putted between the lines of cones and curved slowly around the first turn.

I was turning to wave at Ellen and Jayden when something went "snap" and the go-cart jerked forward.

I gripped the steering wheel and stomped on the brake, but it flapped uselessly. The go-cart went faster and faster, shuddering from the speed. I checked the governor switch. It was flipped up! I tried to push it back down, but it jammed. There was no way I could make the next turn safely.

Beyond the track, the barn doors stood wide open, giving a clear view of the deep meadow on the other side. I held the wheel straight and plowed through the cones toward the barn. The go-cart picked up speed, and by the time I reached the doors, the red building was a blur. I held my breath and steered down the middle of the long barn, and in that instant everything turned black. The go-cart vibrated beneath me, but my staring eyes saw nothing until a pinpoint of light began to grow ahead. I hurtled forward, still clutching the wheel, and shot from the mouth of a tunnel onto a paved road, lined with people.

"Use the brake," someone shouted.

I tried again, and this time it worked. The go-cart slowed, and the engine rumbled to a stop. Mr. Parker ran forward, a huge grin on his face. "We weren't even set up when you came through," he said. "That must be the fastest we've ever found a driver."

Now that the cart was safely stationary, my hands trembled, and I had to take several gasps of breath. I had come to a stop outside the tunnel we used for teleportation on the way to camp.

"It's always a shock the first time," Mr. Parker said cheerfully. "Let's get some bug juice, and you can watch for any others who come through."

I followed him on quivery legs and collapsed in one of the chairs they'd set up for spectators. Sarah was already there, fanning herself with an exotic fan painted with swirls of blue and purple. "Well done," she said. "I always thought how useful it'd be to teleport. I could visit my sister in Missouri whenever I wanted."

"I didn't mean to do it," I said. "My go-cart went out of control, and I steered for the barn to keep from crashing on the curve."

"Hmm, I better tell Mr. Parker."

Mr. Parker shook his head when Sarah spoke with him, then hopped on a go-cart and drove back toward camp. I sat and sipped my drink, waiting for my legs to feel less like rubber.

"Mr. Parker will sort it out," Sarah told me. "Someone must have been playing a joke on you."

"It didn't feel like a joke." My hands had stopped shaking, and now I was feeling mad.

I finished my bug juice as another go-cart blasted from the dark opening and rolled to a stop. Allie, looking pleased, lifted the helmet from her head. I ran to congratulate her.

She gave me a high five. "Two drivers this year," she said. "We usually only find one." She giggled. "Mr. Parker figured out Joanne was the one who tampered with the governor switch and brakes, and she wasn't allowed to try-out."

"He didn't take away more points from the Thornes?" I asked anxiously.

"He gave Ellen back the points Niner took away, but Joanne got ten demerits for the team. On the bright side, you'll get fifty points for transferring through the tunnel."

I wasn't sure there was a bright side to this situation. Joanne would be on the warpath when I saw her next.

The bus arrived to take us back to camp, and Mr. Parker was sitting in front with Joanne glowering by his side.

"Joanne has something to say to you," he said pleasantly.

"I'm sorry I played the joke on you and Ellen. It was supposed to be funny." Her voice didn't sound sorry.

"It's okay," I said, though inside I was simmering.

"Good," Mr. Parker replied, adjusting his green bow tie. "Because I'd like Joanne to be your driving partner. She already has a driver's license, and you will study conventional driving skills at the same time as teleportation."

A flicker of anger rose in Joanne's eyes, but she instantly covered it with a look of superiority. "I'll help the small fry," she said.

The shuttle pulled up at Twain House, and I dashed off before she could say anything else.

Ellen and the others were waiting for me in the dining hall.

"You look like a thundercloud about to burst," she said.

"Yeah—Joanne sabotages my car, and I'm the one who gets punished. I have to take driving class with her."

Ellen must have been giving TJ courage lessons, because she piped up from her end of the table, "We'll ride with you and make sure she doesn't try anything mean."

❧❧

CHAPTER TWELVE

❧❧

That evening, while the fireflies glimmered in the dusk, we spread out through the woods for a huge game of tag. The black outlines of the ancient trees made a lacy canopy over us, and the crickets chirping in the undergrowth seemed to pulse *hurry, hurry*.

Five people were "it," and the Hawthorne elm was our base. I crept through the underbrush, and cries of "home" reached me, as some of the others made it back.

Halfway around the perimeter of the clearing, I scooted under a bush for a better view of the Hawthorne elm. The five had separated, leaving only Ellen to guard the base. She jogged around the clearing, and I made a dash for it when she was on the far side. "Home," I called, and Ellen zoomed around too late.

Snapping twigs made both of us look up. Roy was charging toward the tree, and Ellen turned to chase him. He put on a spurt of speed while the rest of us cheered and squirmed out of the way to give him a clear patch of bark to touch. He crashed into the tree—safe, but his face contorted in pain.

I was closest and saw the terror in his eyes. He collapsed, hugging his knees and trembling uncontrollably.

"Roy's hurt," I yelled. "Get Mr. Parker!"

Jayden took off down the path at a sprint.

"I didn't touch him, I swear," Ellen moaned. "Roy, are you okay?"

But Roy was past hearing. He rocked and shuddered, and nothing we said seemed to reach him.

Mr. Parker arrived, running with Jayden right behind him. He knelt by Roy and took hold of his shoulders. "Roy, listen to me. You must control it. Like TV. Reach out and turn it off."

Roy's body stiffened, and Mr. Parker pressed on his shoulders. "Turn it off, now."

Roy gasped and suddenly relaxed. "It's gone." His voice was barely a whisper, and his face had gone ghostly white. Jayden helped him stand.

"Let's get him inside," Mr. Parker said.

Ivan helped Roy walk, and I told Mr. Parker about the first episode at the lake when Roy saw three boys trying to dunk him in the water.

Roy shivered. "Three boys again. They were pushing me and throwing something above my head. The anger..."

Mr. Parker peered at him, and I knew he was getting the images using his clairvoyance. His face hardened. "He was seeing an event from my years at camp."

A single lamp in the parlor glowed near the couch, and Ivan guided Roy there. He sat, still in a daze, and Mr.

Parker sat down heavily beside him. "You did a fine job turning off the vision."

Roy swallowed. I wasn't sure he felt so confident about it.

"If it happens again, your friends will remind you to shut it off." He motioned to the rest of us to sit down. "It will help if you know the history of what you saw."

I sat on the floor in the pool of light, my back to the dark shadows in the room, and Ivan, TJ, Ellen and Jayden sat around me.

"Are my parents involved?" I asked.

"In a way." Mr. Parker brought the lamp closer to our circle. "I came to camp when I was fifteen, a late bloomer who felt out of place with the younger first-year campers. But there was another kid who was even stranger. His name was Ethan Miller, and he didn't talk. He had a piece of hemp rope he would wind around his hand and twist into a coil. Then he would un-do it and start again. He was too young to be at camp, and I started looking out for him—sitting with him at lunch and helping him with crafts and games."

Mr. Parker stared in the distance, a faint smile on his face, though his eyes were sad. "When I found my power for thought transference, his thoughts hit me like a blast. He came from the past—from Salem—because his mother was hanged as a witch."

He paused and looked at me. "Your parents brought him."

I opened my mouth to start a question, but Mr. Parker shook his head. "I never met them. They left the year before I came, the same year they brought Ethan here. The authorities placed him in foster care in a rural community where his lack of a birth certificate wouldn't be noticed. He was miserable there. But in some ways, camp was worse. Ethan and I were Thornes, and there was a group of Whits who were always ganging up on him. One day they cornered Ethan under the Hawthorne elm while he was winding his rope. They took it from him, and when I ran to help, they started a game of keep-away. I could feel Ethan's anger raging, and I was afraid he was going to crack."

"Is that what Roy saw?"

"Yes. One of the kids who caught the rope was an empath, and he yelped like he'd been burned."

Mr. Parker paused as though considering whether he should continue. "The rope was a piece from the noose that hanged Ethan's mother."

"Poor Ethan," TJ said.

Mr. Parker sighed. "I got the rope back and told Ethan it wasn't safe anymore, but he seemed suddenly cold. He let me bury it under the old elm, but he never confided in me again. He started talking at last and discovered his own gift for thought transference. But he always kept his distance, and his strangeness frightened the other campers. I should have been glad he wasn't picked on anymore, but I missed our old friendship. I always felt that when I hid that rope, I hid away something of Ethan."

Roy sat forward. "What happened to him?"

"He was unusually brilliant, and the year I was head counselor, he won a scholarship to study physics at Harvard. I didn't see him again until Lindsey showed me her impressions from the kidnapping last summer. Ethan had taken back his original name."

Mr. Parker looked at me, his forehead knit together. "His mother's name was Temperance Card, and Ethan Miller became Dr. Card."

"Dr. Card?" I shivered, remembering his cold eyes staring into mine, the fingers of his thoughts probing at my brain. He kidnapped our entire camp last year in his frenzied pursuit of a time machine that my parents had used.

He was also responsible for their deaths.

CHAPTER THIRTEEN

The next day, Roy joined us at lunch, his eyes shining behind his thick glasses. "I had a great class with the empaths today," he announced. "Mr. Parker asked our teacher to show us how to block impressions, and then we practiced with all kinds of things. I'm not good with objects, but if I'm inside something, it works. She brought an old pilot seat from the plane Lindbergh flew, and you wouldn't believe the views from the air. I got the knack for turning it off, too. It's like when you first look in a room before you enter, you can always back out."

I'd never heard Roy say so many words at once. The way he lifted his head and gazed confidently around the group—he seemed like he'd grown up a year or two.

I wasn't feeling as confident after my lesson with Aunt Winnie. With driving try-outs and Roy's crisis, I hadn't done any practice. She pursed her lips together, and the wrinkles in her forehead grew deeper under the cloud of white hair. "You have to work if you want this gift," she said.

She made me go through the same exercises as the day before, and though I tried to concentrate, I didn't make any progress. "Work harder," she said at the end of class.

After lunch Ellen pulled me aside. "Mr. Parker wants to meet at his office," she whispered. "I recorded all the strange words, like you asked, and he wants to see the notebook."

Jayden was hanging around near us. "I never get to see you," he said shyly. "Can we meet at the Junction Stone after your meeting?"

I felt a blush growing on my cheeks. "I'll see you there," I promised.

The rest of camp had a free swim, but we got permission from Skeeter to see Mr. Parker. "Don't forget your first driving lesson later on," she said cheerily.

I groaned. A driving lesson with Joanne would be pure misery. I rushed back and told Jayden we'd have to meet after the driving lesson.

He shrugged, like the meeting was my idea. "That's cool."

Ellen and I reported to Mr. Parker's office at Twain House. The only furnishings were three shabby chairs and a desk with one leg propped with the P and Q encyclopedias. Photos from past sessions of camp covered the walls. In one faded picture a group of campers clustered around a squirrel, who was posing for the camera. In another, five kids grinned as they held a car above their heads.

"Aren't these your parents?" Ellen asked, pointing to a snapshot of six students holding a poster with the words "SBI Fellowship Award." In their midst my dad waved at the camera while my mom stood dreamily looking into the distance, almost like she could see us. I stepped closer and looked into her eyes, wishing she really could.

Mr. Parker arrived and the desk chair creaked as he sat down. "Thanks for coming. I wanted a safe place where we could talk since the roofers are here. The SBI made the arrangements, but I don't trust the crew. Their foreman didn't know the nature of this camp, and I'd like to keep it that way."

"What's the SBI?"

"Your parents worked for them—the Scientific Bureau of Investigation. Similar to the FBI but a focus on psychic phenomenon. They're the ones tracking Dr. Card."

"They haven't found him yet?"

"No, and I'm beginning to think they never will. He's discovered some way to cloak his whereabouts. But enough of that, Aunt Winnie said I need to get an update from you two."

I told him how worried I was about Lindsey—how she'd sent a letter but my efforts to help her didn't bring solid answers. I described the fuzzy impressions I got of the tunnel lined with earth and the diagram in the attic.

"And you've had more of these odd sentences?" he asked Ellen.

She brought out her notebook and read them for us. The lines flowed like poetry, though not all the same rhythm. Beautiful words too, like *blossomed* and *stars.*

"Wait, read that last one again," I said.

Ellen read: *"Where all parting, pain, and care, and death and time shall disappear."*

"That's it! The poem about the clock—all these lines are from Longfellow's poems." I almost bounced out of the rickety chair. "There's only one person who quotes his poetry like that—Lindsey."

Ellen's eyes grew wide. "Could Lindsey have a mind link with my braces?"

"Long-distance links are unusual." He frowned and tapped a pencil on his desk. "I'm going to pick up Lindsey this afternoon, but I'm a little concerned. No one answered the phone when I called her family to confirm her location."

He peered at Ellen. "Could you try to reach out to whoever is sending those messages—something simple like 'Are you there?' If it's Lindsey, we can get her location."

Ellen's face clouded. "I'm not a clairvoyant, you know."

He laughed. "But you do have braces with some unusual properties. If Lindsey's thoughts can reach you, then she ought to be able to pick up your thoughts."

Ellen closed her eyes. "I'll give it a try."

We waited, but after a few minutes she sighed. "Nothing. Not even the static. It usually comes at night."

"Keep trying throughout the day," he said.

After our meeting, Ellen walked with me to the field behind Whittier House for my driving lesson. TJ came with us as she had promised.

Unfortunately, the car was a tiny two-seater.

"No room," Joanne smirked, "unless you want to ride in the trunk."

Niner handed me the keys. "Remember, no dashing off this time."

He obviously didn't believe the go-cart was sabotaged.

"I'll take care of her, sir." Joanne smiled at him, but the moment he turned away she muttered under her breath, "I'm going to make your life a horror."

I nervously put the key in the ignition. Grandma didn't have a car, but Lindsey's mom used to drive us around a lot. I tried to think what she did. I turned the key, and the car coughed to life but then went quiet. I twisted the key again, and a sound like knives in a garbage disposal made me jump.

"The car's already started," Joanne yelled.

I snatched back my hand. "How am I supposed to know?" I shouted back.

"I can't believe I'm teaching a baby to drive." She grudgingly showed me how to put the car in drive and where the accelerator and brakes were. "And this is the emergency brake," she said, patting a long black lever between us. "Don't make me use it."

I tried my strategy from the go-carts of barely pressing the accelerator and letting the car roll forward, but Joanne shouted "press harder." Fortunately they had widened the cones in the track. I slowly wobbled between the lines and tried adding a little speed. The moment I did, the car lurched forward, flattening some cones.

Joanne clutched the dashboard. "Stupid—you're going to get us killed!"

I looked out of the corner of my eye. Niner was watching from the side while he talked with Skeeter, who would be teaching Allie. They were standing next to an old beat-up station wagon. I wished I had class with them.

A few more cones bit the dust, and every time I wandered off course Joanne went crazy, but I began enjoying the lesson. It was like pinching her in the arm, and she couldn't do anything about it.

I relaxed back in my seat and squinted into the sun. Driving wasn't so bad. The meadow stretched before me, dotted with buttercups. In the distance the woods were a dark smudge under the bright sky. They blurred for a moment, and I saw the earthen tunnel again and a glimpse of a room, lined with rock that sparkled by the light of a lantern.

"Where are you going?" Joanne barked.

The image disappeared, and I found myself barreling across the meadow, way outside the track of cones, my foot pressing the accelerator. I panicked and pressed harder on the pedal, and the car hit a rut and bounced us in the air.

"Hit the brake!"

I stomped on the other pedal, and at the same time Joanne pulled on the emergency brake, and the car jerked to a stop. My chest hit the steering wheel, knocking the wind out of me.

"That's it—I quit." Joanne tore off the seatbelt and stormed from the car. I heard her yelling at Niner. "She's crazy—You can't expect me to risk my life!"

My head throbbed, and my heart was going faster than a race car, but I didn't know how to turn off the car. I sat with my foot on the brake, listening to the rumble of the engine, and trying to catch my breath.

Skeeter came at last. "Going for some off-road driving?" she asked with a chuckle.

She reached in the car to set it to "park" and turned off the ignition. "Not too bad for a twelve-year-old driver. You'll do better next time."

But I was determined there wouldn't be a next time. It wasn't safe to drive if possibilities were going to wobble in front of my eyes. I stumbled out of the car, my legs still jittery. I had to swallow before my voice worked. "I saw something out there," I said. "That's why I drove so wild." I told Skeeter about the picture of the tunnel and the room with glittery rocks in the walls.

"You need to tell Mr. Parker," she said. "And I'll tell Niner that I'm teaching you next time," she added with a wink.

I was so worried about reporting on the image that I forgot Jayden wanted to meet at the Junction Stone. I waited at Mr. Parker's office for a half hour before I remembered he was planning to pick up Lindsey that afternoon.

I figured she had probably arrived at Hawthorne House, so I started off to meet her. I ran into Jayden at the Junction Stone, and I suddenly remembered.

"Sorry I'm late, I—"

"Niner says it shows disrespect," Jayden said.

"Disrespect?"

"When you're late."

"There's a reason I'm late." I stopped. Jayden would probably blame me for forgetting our meeting. "Never mind. You don't really think I disrespect you?"

Jayden stared back, his eyes half-closed. "Niner says actions talk."

Prickles of heat spread up my neck, and I felt my face burning. If I heard another word about Niner I was going to explode.

"At Boot Camp, we—"

"I'm not listening!" I turned my back on him and walked at a furious pace down the trail to the lake. If he wasn't going to be reasonable, he would miss hearing about all that happened today.

❧

I finally found Mr. Parker in his office just before dinner. When he heard about the image of the rock-lined room, he ran his fingers through his hair so that it stood up on end. "We're missing something here," he said.

"Something that links these phenomena." He pulled a paper from his desk. "I went to pick up Lindsey, and she wasn't there. I contacted the SBI, and they found Lindsey's parents—on vacation in Florida. They thought she was here at camp. That means she's been missing for six days."

Six days! And all that time I hadn't done a thing to help. I felt the panic rising in my throat. "What can we do?"

"I'll tell the SBI about your visions," he said. "They're following every lead."

Allie burst into the office. "Mr. Parker, Niner needs you at Longfellow House right away."

We took off at a run. Allie was already breathless, but she managed to tell us what happened. "We found Niner in the attic—knocked out and tied up with rope—and the roofers gone."

Niner, a purple bruise above his eye, was poking around the big room outside the attic with his clipboard in hand. He scowled at me, and I figured he didn't want to make his report in front of an audience.

"Can't believe they got the jump on me, sir," he said. "But Allie was alert when I didn't return and found me almost immediately. As far as I can tell, nothing is missing. They searched the trunk and desk over there, but everything else is in place."

"What were they doing when you found them?"

"Looking at the attic floor, but I didn't see much before they knocked me out."

"Show me."

Niner led the way to the attic. Someone had polished the diagram on the floor so that more details appeared, including needle-thin etchings of initials.

I studied the pattern of diamonds and squares, but the possibilities refused to kick in. Why would the roofers care about this diagram? And why attack Niner?

I found Ellen at dinner and told her everything. She was especially worried about Lindsey. "We've got to do what we can to help," she said.

While the others went to the evening camp fire, we sat in the parlor at Hawthorne House, waiting for Ellen to get a new sentence. The portrait of the old colonel glowered down on us, and Ellen sketched a new smiling version in her notebook. "He looks much better, don't you think?" She squinted at the portrait. "I think he'd be smiling if he could see how his house is used now."

The quiet parlor was perfect for practicing possibilities. I brought up images of the diagram and Revere's trunk and tried to get them to develop. I concentrated so hard my head ached.

"Anything?" Ellen asked.

"No."

"Me either." She abandoned her sketching and sat tensely staring out the window. When the sounds of returning campers echoed on the steps, she was almost in tears. "It wouldn't be so bad if Mr. Parker didn't need my help."

"Maybe it will come while you're sleeping," I said.

"Let's try a little longer."

We waited until the house was quiet and everyone in bed, then we crept upstairs and into our bunks. A feeling of heaviness settled in my gut. Lindsey needed us, and we weren't any closer to finding her.

I fell asleep, and the nightmare came again. My parents in a car, going too fast—careening down a hill. I yelled for them to stop, but they didn't seem to hear. My father was laughing and my mother was singing a song. *Listen, listen, listen…* A flash of light exploded in front of the car, and I woke up.

My heart was thudding in my chest and my pillowcase was wet. I took slow deep breaths, fighting the weight of blackness and despair. I was powerless to save my parents. What hope was there that I could help Lindsey?

✣✣

CHAPTER FOURTEEN

✣✣

Breakfast the next morning seemed quiet. The details of Niner's attack had spread throughout camp, but everyone seemed scared to talk about it. Ellen didn't talk at all. She carried her notebook and pen with her and jumped when I said her name.

"I'll find Mr. Parker today," she said. "I'll tell him the sentences have stopped."

"It's only been a day," I said, but she shook her head.

I had driving class this morning instead of Aunt Winnie's lessons, and at first I felt relieved. After the horrible dream last night, I wasn't sure I wanted to practice. Then I felt guilty about shirking her class. I promised myself to work extra-hard tomorrow.

Skeeter found me before the driving lesson. "Wear sunglasses," she told me. "It will cut down on those visions. The camp store sells them if you don't have any."

Fortunately I had sunglasses. Grandma thought of everything when she helped me pack. I walked back to Hawthorne House to get them. The day was already growing warm, and I was dimly aware of the hum of insects from the creek that followed the path.

I was thinking about Ellen and her worries over the strange sentences when I heard a muffled static coming from behind a rock. It was a tiny pink mp3 player, the ear buds sputtering and murmuring. I remembered the awful music during our dorm party. It must belong to Joanne. I couldn't believe she let her precious music out of her sight.

I twirled the dial to turn down the volume, but I must have activated something else because a tiny radio voice spoke from the ear buds. "That was Radio WV14 and another classic..."

"What are you doing?"

I spun around to see Niner standing squarely in front of me, arms crossed.

"I...I just found this behind the rock."

He yanked the player from my hands. "Not likely. I had reports there was music at Hawthorne House several nights ago, and here's proof. Twenty demerits from the Thornes."

"But it's not mine—"

"You know the rule—no electronic devices at camp. Especially anything with a radio receiver." His eyes narrowed. "I'm reporting this to Mr. Parker." He strode off down the path.

I was so mad, blue dots swirled in front of my eyes. Niner never listened and always assumed the worst. If only he knew it was really Joanne who had an mp3 player! A rush of anger surged through my brain. For once I was going to tell Joanne exactly what I thought of her. I sprinted the rest of the way to Hawthorne House and burst through the front door into a cluster of kids hanging out in the camp store.

"Whoa," said Jayden. "You could be lethal with that door."

Joanne was behind the counter, taking money and passing out granola bars and T-shirts to a line of kids. I pushed my way to the front.

She tossed her dark hair over her shoulder and gave me her superior stare. "You'll have to wait your turn."

"I'm not waiting for anything," I shouted. "You put our whole camp in jeopardy with your stupid music. No electronic devices, remember?"

Joanne froze for an instant, but quickly recovered and put on a sickly sweet smile. "There must be some mistake," she murmured.

Jayden was pulling me by the elbow but I shook him off. "There's no mistake. I was in the dorm when you played your awful music."

"Annaliese, Destiny, did you see any electronic devices in our dorm?" Her voice was still sugary, but her eyes locked with mine.

The other girls giggled. "We didn't see anything."

"Come on," Jayden said. This time he pulled me away from the counter and out the door. He must have used his telekinetic powers because my feet barely touched the floor.

He set me down under the Hawthorne elm. "You've gotta get over this," he said. "You're picking fights with Joanne, and it's going to get worse."

I couldn't believe he was taking *her* side. "Leave me alone!" I took off running toward the Junction Stone.

"Stella, come back," Jayden called, but I pretended I didn't hear.

I forgot my sunglasses, but Skeeter loaned me hers. Driving class was so difficult I had to put everything else out of my mind—Joanne's nastiness, Niner's injustice, and Jayden not understanding. Especially Jayden. I got a stomach ache when I thought of him.

Skeeter was a great teacher. She taught me how to start the car properly and brake gently so we weren't thrown forward. Before the hour was over, I could put the car in reverse and make a three point turn. We even parked at the end. I drove the station wagon, which moved more slowly than the two-seater I used yesterday. By the end of class I felt better about driving and life in general. Until I saw Jayden at lunch.

He frowned when I arrived and left to sit with the guys from Longfellow House.

"What's going on?" TJ asked.

"Jayden has some crazy idea that he needs to keep me from fighting with Joanne."

"Maybe he's trying to protect you," she said.

I gritted my teeth. "I don't think so."

Ellen joined us and wanted to know why we were down twenty points on the team chart. Her voice turned shrill when she heard about the mp3 player. "Of all the cheap tricks—I bet Joanne planted it so you'd get in trouble."

That sounded like Joanne, but then she was in our dorm and stood to lose points too. Would she risk demerits for the petty satisfaction of picking on me? It was more likely she dropped it on accident, but all the same—I got the blame!

The CITs hosted a card party during the afternoon. They chose fast-paced games that didn't give the clairvoyants time to read the other players' cards. I was too tired to play so I sat off to the side and watched.

The telekinetics dealt the cards without using their hands, so it looked like a mini-cyclone spitting cards at the players.

I tried not to look at Jayden, who was probably the best of the bunch. I used to be proud of him, but now he just irritated me. He thought Niner was always right, and he didn't believe ME, his oldest friend in the world. I needed to prove to him that I was innocent, and I suddenly had an idea of someone who could help—Roy.

I intercepted him on the stairs at Hawthorne House as he came down for dinner.

"Me?" Roy squeaked when I told him my plan.

"You can hold the mp3 player and tell me its story."

"You forget that my gift only works when I'm *in* a place."

"Okay, we'll take it to the rock where I found it, and then you can tell me about it.

His eyes fluttered rapidly behind his glasses, and his face looked slightly green. "I'm sure Niner has a rule about this."

I kicked the bottom step. "That's the problem with Niner—too many rules."

Roy was hyperventilating by the time we reached Twain House. I pulled him down the hall to Niner's room. "Remember, if anyone interrupts us, we'll say you came to ask Niner a question," I said.

Roy's ears turned red. "What if they think we're sneaking around kissing, like Joanne and…"

I pushed him toward the door. "Let 'em think it!" The more he dithered, the more determined I got.

"Th-this is Niner's room," Roy said.

A single cot with the blanket neatly tucked around the mattress stood in the corner. Beside it was a dresser with a comb, toothbrush and toothpaste lined up in a row.

I pulled open the top drawer and found socks rolled in tight balls, arranged in columns with military precision, but no mp3 player. The second drawer was filled with T-shirts lined up like sausages. Again nothing. The bottom drawer was full of pocket notebooks bundled with rubber bands. Without thinking, I flipped one open and saw *0900 Dining Hall Surveillance*. It gave me the creeps, and I quickly returned it to the stack. In the back corner lay the mp3 player. "Got it."

"What are you doing here?"

I jumped and looked up. Jayden stood in the doorway. "I was looking for you," he began. His gaze flicked from Roy to me and then to the bottom drawer, which hung open with notebooks heaped to one side. The mp3 player felt like a scorching coal in my hands.

"I'm going to prove that I'm right," I said, lifting my chin in the air.

Jayden took a step toward me, holding out his hand for the device. "Why don't you trust Niner?"

"Why doesn't he trust me?" I countered. I pressed the mp3 player into Roy's hands. "Roy's going to tell us the truth."

"But I'm…" Roy's voice trailed off.

Jayden levitated the player from his hands. "You think you're above the rules, Stella." He returned the device to the drawer and closed it with a snap. "How can you ask me to believe you when you do things like this?"

I couldn't talk. The breath was knocked out of me like the time I fell off the uneven bars in gym class. My face burning, I pushed past Jayden and out of the room, squeezing my eyes shut to hold back the tears.

୰ଡ଼ଡ଼

CHAPTER FIFTEEN

୰ଡ଼ଡ଼

I slammed out the front door and almost tripped over a bike left on the porch. Skeeter's bike. She'd invited us to use it, and suddenly it seemed like a wonderful idea. On a bike, I could go far, far away. I wouldn't have to face all the questions at dinner or Jayden's accusations.

I pedaled down the Twain driveway and took the turn toward the highway, pumping the pedals until my legs burned. Bits of gravel flew out from the wheels, and the jolting over the trail shook up the rage inside me.

I skittered around the curves, pushing myself faster, and after a last sharp crook in the trail, the log arch at the camp entrance came into view. I imagined a white banner stretching across the opening, like police tape at a crime scene. It read "NINER'S RULES" in black letters. I sped toward it. The bike hit the curb at the highway's edge, flying into the air for a moment, and I broke through the entrance. No more rules!

The smooth surface of the highway sent the bike rolling faster and faster. I reached the top of a hill, and below lay the tunnel we used for teleportation. The black entrance drew me—the perfect place to lose myself. I accelerated toward it, feeling like a comet, my anger burning a trail behind me.

The bike flew through the entrance at top speed, and I gasped at the sudden darkness. It wasn't the darkness of night. It was utter blackness—the blackness of teleporting. I felt a surge of power. I was leaving camp behind, making my own way. I squeezed the handle bars and kept pedaling like crazy, putting into it all my resentment—Niner taking Joanne's side, Niner luring Jayden into his schemes, Niner making my life a misery of rules, rules, rules.

The faster I pushed the pedals, the darker and colder the tunnel grew. I felt the anger leaking out of me and a new calmness growing. I thought about the one place I really wanted to be right now—home.

A tiny point of light gleamed ahead, growing to the size of a sparkling Christmas ornament, and then a glowing lamp, and finally a distant exit from the tunnel. I coasted the last twenty yards and shot into the glare of summer.

It took my eyes a minute to adjust, but when they did, I saw Perkins Lane running behind my school and looking back—Old Simmons Tunnel. I did it!

My heart fluttered, and I did a few laps around the school parking lot, savoring my new independence. Niner couldn't boss me around anymore. I had an escape.

I glided down Williams Road toward my house, and it was odd to see ordinary life going on—people mowing their lawns and kids running through sprinklers. One car passed slowly, and a toddler in the back seat pointed at me, but to everyone else I seemed invisible. None of them knew how amazing it was that I was *here*, biking down the street. I wondered if this was what ghosts felt like.

Our street was quiet. Miss Charlotte would probably be at one of her many jobs, and Grandma would usually be reading in her recliner at this time of day.

I parked my bike and ran up to the front door, bursting to surprise Grandma. But when I turned the knob, it was locked. We never locked the door.

Something didn't seem right, and I realized what it was—all the windows were shut, and the house was dark.

Feeling like a burglar at my own home, I tried the side window on the porch. It rose stiffly, and I swung a leg over the windowsill to duck inside. The living room smelled of dust and heat, like a room that had been closed up for a long time.

I turned on the lights as I moved through the house. Everything was too tidy—no open letters lying around, no books face-down on chairs. Grandma's bed was made, and the roses I left in her vase were gone.

I checked the refrigerator for a note. We left messages there for each other, but I only found the purple pig magnets I got Grandma for her birthday. I was tempted to write "I miss you" and stick it under a magnet, but it might scare her when she got back.

Dusk was falling, and I had to leave without seeing Grandma. I started the ride back to Old Simmons Tunnel feeling strangely flat. There must be an explanation for

Grandma not being home. Miss Charlotte would have written me if anything was wrong. But I worried anyway.

The transfer through the tunnel back to camp was much harder. My muscles ached from the first angry dash, and my mind felt floaty, like I was hovering somewhere above the bike. I realized I should have eaten something when I stopped by Grandma's house, or at least gotten some water.

I leaned over the handlebars and willed my legs to keep pumping the pedals. The light in the tunnel turned gray, then came the darkness of a moonlit night, then, as though a candle had been snuffed out, a cold, thick blackness surrounded me.

It lasted so long I seemed to fall asleep, cycling on and on. At last a pin point of light appeared, and I kept steadily toward it. I had to push to finish the last stretch, reminding myself I had a secret escape now.

The light didn't grow, and I soon discovered the reason. Night had fallen, and the glow came from the street lamp that stood outside the tunnel. My legs were wobbly, and my fingers numb on the handlebars by the time I reached it.

I slowly pushed the bike up the hill, draining the last of my energy. At the top I got back on the bike and let it coast to the Camp Hawthorne sign. It swung gently, creaking on its chain.

In the moonlight, the trail was a pale strip, swallowed by overhanging branches of pine and oak. The hooting of an owl startled me, and I held my breath as I started down the path, hoping a light from Twain House would find me before the shadows engulfed me entirely.

In the darkness, someone started singing. The song was faint, but I knew the voice. It was TJ singing *Listen, listen, listen for me*. I followed the song down the path, pedaling slowly in time to the tune, the soft moonlight like a dream.

At the Junction Stone TJ stood with her hand on the rock, gazing up at the starry sky. She stopped singing when I skittered up on the bike. "I was waiting for you," she said.

Two people sat at her feet. They rose up, and a flashlight clicked on to reveal Ellen and Roy.

"We have something to show you," Ellen said, taking hold of my hand. Roy took her other hand and TJ began to sing. A vision blossomed in my mind. I looked at Roy, and his eyes were vacant, staring at something far away.

"Watch," he said.

I saw the Junction Stone as the sun was setting, turning the clouds bright orange. A small boy stood between two older kids—my parents.

My dad had his hand on the boy's shoulder. "Ethan, I want you to nod if you understand what we're saying."

The boy looked at the ground.

My mom knelt beside him. "We're going away for a while. Do you understand?"

He remained frozen.

"Your mother wanted us to bring you here," she continued, and Ethan looked up for the first time. "Where we're going, we might be able to help you. We'll do everything we can. I promise."

She hugged Ethan and two tears traced lines down his cheeks.

"We have to get the bus now, but we'll see you soon."

My parents walked away from Ethan, holding hands. My heart pounded to a stop, and I gasped for air. I wanted to run after them and tell them to come back. I wanted to feel their hands touching me. I wanted to look in their eyes and see them looking back.

They disappeared in the dusk on the path to Twain House, and Ethan lifted his head and cried an unearthly howl. It expressed all the loss and grief I knew.

The vision was replaced with darkness, and warm arms clasped me. "Come back, Stella," TJ said.

❧❧

CHAPTER SIXTEEN

❧❧

I couldn't sleep that night. I kept dreaming of my parents talking with Ethan Card. Sometimes I would join them, other times not. But every time it ended with them walking away and Ethan's howl of loss. I woke up over and over, chilled with sweat.

I lay in my bunk and watched the gray light of dawn illuminate the tangled branches of the Hawthorne elm. The vision of my parents bothered me more deeply than I expected. It wasn't only my own grief that came surging back, but Ethan Card's as well. I couldn't accept it.

Until this summer, all I knew about Dr. Card was that he stole the time machine and had ultimately killed my parents. I wasn't prepared for the idea that …he loved them.

At breakfast I sat by myself, too tired to talk with my friends. Ivan found me anyway. He pulled up a chair and leaned over, a scheming gleam in his eye. "I heard you had a tough time last night." He shook his head like an old grandfather, tsk-tsking over a youngster. "Nothing like a little research to cheer you up, eh?"

I listlessly turned over a pancake on my plate, not even meeting his eyes, but Ivan plunged ahead.

"What you need is more information on the Lindsey-problem, and thanks to the address on your letter, I found her farm on a map in the Twain library. Townsend Mine sits right next to it."

The piece of paper we found in George Washington's desk popped in my mind. " *--nd Mine, 355*," I murmured.

"Righto," Ivan replied. He lit a finger and warmed up the toast on his plate. "And I found out it's a rhodium mine."

A prickle of interest broke through the numbness in my brain.

Ivan waved to Ellen, who scurried over, carrying a thick notebook. "I've got more information for you," she said.

I raised my eyebrows, and she giggled. "Don't look so shocked—research is one thing I can still do."

She opened the notebook and flipped through page after page of notes copied in tiny handwriting. "Rhodium was discovered in 1803 and is found mixed with other metals like silver, nickel, copper, or gold.

"Valuable?" Ivan asked.

"Immensely—it's one of the rarest elements on earth, and it looks like silver. It's called a noble metal because it doesn't corrode, and it conducts electricity really well. Oh, and burning is required to obtain rhodium in its pure form."

Ivan cupped a ball of fire in his hands. "That's my department."

"Great research," I said, and Ellen glowed.

The gong sounded to signal classes beginning soon.

Somehow, Ivan and Ellen had cleared the fog of sadness swirling in my mind.

"I've got to run or I'll be late, but let me know if you find out more," I said.

Aunt Winnie was still in bed when I arrived. I'd rarely seen her anywhere but her wheelchair, rolling energetically around her cabin, tending to the chickens or watering flowers.

"I'm not feeling well today," she said, with a sigh. "Getting old." She fixed me with her sharp gaze. "You figure out the possibilities yet?"

"No—" I stopped. The truth was I hadn't made any progress yesterday—hadn't even practiced.

She squinted at me. "You're letting things distract you. How will you use the possibilities if you don't work?"

I dropped into the chair next to her bed. "Couldn't you take care of them? You've got loads more experience than me."

"My possibilities are completely different from yours," she snapped.

"What do you see?"

"The need to teach you as much as possible before…" She paused and laid her hand on mine. It seemed thin and frail, like a brown leaf that might blow away in the wind.

"Promise me you will practice." She closed her eyes. "You may go now."

I left Aunt Winnie's cabin, worry churning in my gut. She was my last link to my parents, and her frailty scared me. She'd taught my dad incredible powers—I'd seen them with my own eyes—so why wasn't my gift coming easier? Now that we knew Lindsey was missing, the pressure was worse. A heavy feeling settled in my chest. I tried to take a deep breath but my lungs had forgotten how to work.

At lunch Roy was sitting by himself, building an immense sandwich with layers of turkey and cheese on rye bread.

"Where are the others?" I asked.

"Niner has the boot camp kids running extra laps."

I helped myself to some bread and started assembling my own sandwich—cheese with lettuce and salsa. I kept my eyes on the bread. After last night I felt shy around Roy.

"You okay?" he asked, peering at me from behind his glasses.

I swallowed the sadness welling up again. "I didn't know you could do that—link people to your visions. It was…"

"Overwhelming?"

"Yeah."

"That's the way it is for me, too."

We munched in silence for a few minutes, but I had a question I needed to ask. "Do you think there are more scenes with my parents?"

He turned as red as the salsa. "I saw their first kiss under the Hawthorne elm."

"Not that kind of thing." I laughed nervously. I wasn't exactly sure what I wanted. Roy's visions seemed to be connected to moments of intense emotion. Was I ready for that?

He finished his sandwich and began building a second one. "I can take you around. I've always thought there'd be stuff around the lake, but I didn't want to try alone."

"Can you choose the time you want to see?"

"No—I just turn off the visions I don't want to watch." He blushed again. "That's what I did for the kiss."

We left before the others arrived, and Roy stopped me halfway down the trail. He checked the trees around us before he spoke. "I wanted to get you out here so I could tell you something else. I found out I can receive impressions from objects, and I got something from the mp3 player before Jayden took it away."

"Was it Joanne's?"

"No, it belonged to the roofers."

"The roofers?" That was a whole new problem. "Did you tell Niner?"

"I was afraid to. He wouldn't like me going through his stuff."

"At least tell Mr. Parker, okay?"

Roy's eyes shifted away from me. "I'll try," he said.

We walked on, but I didn't feel as jubilant as I thought I'd be over the proof of my innocence. Now I had to admit I was wrong about Joanne. What would Jayden say? Probably tell me I was as bad as Niner—jumping to conclusions.

We walked around the lake, but Roy didn't find any memories of my parents. I was ready to give up when I had a brilliant idea for a place to go.

Last year the Thornes dug in a field that had unusual artifacts. Later we learned that my parents used the place for their time portal, which caused the odd mix of objects found there. If any place would hold memories of my parents, that would be the one.

We had to walk a long way to the dig site, and I began to worry what Roy might see. I wondered if my possibilities were kicking in or whether it was just my usual fears. But when we arrived, Roy froze before the patch of ground marked off for the dig.

"What are you seeing?" I put my hand on his arm, and then I saw it, too.

A boy and girl staggered through a lightning storm, carrying a burden between them. They sank to the ground, and I saw that it was my parents, and they were carrying a little boy—Ethan Card. His eyes were closed, and he was clutching a coil of rope.

My mother tried to tear it from his fingers, sobbing in gasps as the rain pelted around them. "I can't get it from him," she shouted over the roll of thunder.

My dad held her by the shoulders and brought his face close to hers. "He needs to keep it." He looked up, and his eyes seemed to flicker over us for a moment.

Lightning flashed around him, and he took out a knife and sawed at the rope until a short length separated from the rest. The effort seemed to exhaust him, and he staggered to the center of the dig site. "I leave this here for you," he shouted. "You must keep it safe."

With a last rumble of thunder, the vision faded as quickly as it had appeared, but the rope remained, half submerged in the dirt. Roy, his face pale, walked as though in a trance and picked it up.

His body stiffened. "Your parents didn't arrive in time. They were supposed to save Temperance Card, but the mob got there first. They tied her to a tree…"

He dropped the rope as though it burned his fingers. "I won't see anymore."

His words hit me like a punch in the gut. Was this why Dr. Card pursued his insane quest for power—to avenge his mother?

I realized I was crying, tears rolling down my cheeks. I picked up the rope, and the ache in my stomach seemed to multiply by a hundred.

I'd grown used to fearing and hating Dr. Card, but Roy's visions were changing my ideas about him, and I didn't like how it felt.

৵৽

CHAPTER SEVENTEEN

৵৽

After dinner Niner called everyone outside for a game of Capture-the-Flag. Roy's vision still haunted my thoughts. I rested my hand on the piece of rope in my pocket, hoping the game would give me the time I needed to work out what I'd seen.

We gathered in the far field behind Longfellow House. Thick forest surrounded the clearing, but on one side the woods gave way to dozens of overgrown apple trees planted behind the house. The setting sun gilded the distant rooftop, giving it the strange appearance of rising in the middle of a wilderness.

Niner wore his tricorn hat from the Paul Revere play and swaggered in front of the teams. "Twains and Whits on one side, and Thornes, Alcotts and Fellows on the other," he bellowed in his megaphone voice. "For this game we will have the Brits and the Patriots—like the American Revolution."

He held up a blue flag with a red X on it, and presented it to Skeeter. "The Brits will guard this flag and protect the territory from here into the woods." He gave Eugene the second flag—blue with a circle of stars. "And the

Patriots will guard this flag on the other side, which includes the boundary to General Washington's headquarters at Longfellow House. The limits are marked with blue paint on the trees." He paused and looked directly at me. "Stay within bounds at all time. Let the game begin—"

Eugene charged for the woods near Longfellow House. "Patriots to me!"

We sprinted after him. He didn't stop until he reached a spot where the trees grew thick.

"Speed is the secret of this game," he growled. "We need someone to guard the flag, who can move position from tree to tree." Jayden volunteered, and Eugene clapped him on the back. "Next we need a secure prison."

One of the Alcotts volunteered to make it, and Eugene assigned their team as prison-keepers.

"Now for offense," he said, the spark of war in his eye.

His plan was to use every spare man to infiltrate enemy lines by any means possible, leaving a minimum of Patriots to capture the Brits. I wasn't sure it would work, but it was more fun than sitting around waiting for them to sneak past us. Capture-the-Flag was like a two-sided game of tag, and I was pretty good at not getting caught.

It was a relief to have Jayden off on his own mission. He tried to say something to me before he left with the flag, but I wouldn't look at him.

I began creeping toward the enemy line and realized TJ was shadowing me. Drat! How was I going to be invisible with an extra scout on my tail?

I stopped and motioned for her to be quiet, but she scooted forward and began whispering. "Roy has an idea."

I peered into the dusk and saw Roy a few steps behind her. "This is not the time for a chat," I whispered.

He must have taken my stopping as his cue, and he scurried forward through the underbrush. "Remember how the roofers searched Paul Revere's trunk?" His face was earnest, his eyes wide behind his round glasses. "If I could get in the trunk, I might learn something."

"It would mean breaking the rules again," I said.

He swallowed. "I'm ready."

"Lead on."

Eugene had stationed Ellen as lookout, and she intercepted us before we made it to the apple trees. "What are you doing here?" she demanded. "You're supposed to be advancing on the enemy."

"Roy has an idea about Revere's trunk," I began. "Let us pass, and—"

"Good! Anything's better than hanging around here with nothing to do," Ellen interrupted. "I'll go with you."

Our group was growing too large, and I worried we'd be stopped and questioned, but Eugene's strategy to send everyone on offense worked to our advantage. We reached the blue marks at the boundary line without any trouble. A delicious sense of victory made my arms tingle—I was going to cross the line and break one of Niner's rules.

I paused and looked back. Jayden sat high in a tree, watching us. He glowered down at me and shook his head, but I turned away and raced toward the apple orchard. The others followed.

The ancient apple trees formed an archway of branches over us, leading to the tidy lawn that surrounded the house like a green blanket. The sun had set, and Longfellow House glowed serenely in the moonlight, the windows dark and mysterious.

We let ourselves in the door, making our way with TJ's flashlight, and I led the way to the back stairs. Desks and bulky chairs cast shadows on the wall, and TJ drew closer to me. "You don't suppose the roofers will return, do you?"

"No, Mr. Parker said once they left, they can't find their way back."

"But what if they never left?"

The steps creaked as we climbed to the attic. "Don't think about it," I said.

The piles were just as we left them, though the trunk lid had been closed. Roy shivered as I opened it.

"I'm going to do this," he said.

He jumped inside and sank down to sit with knees clasped, staring ahead. His voice, when it came, sounded thin and faraway. "Paul Revere rescued this trunk, and George Washington tells him the enemy mustn't find it, or all will be lost. It's not the papers inside that are valuable…it's the… lining."

Roy paused and his face looked confused. "The diagram. For some reason that's important... 355 knows. She's the center of it with Revere."

His eyes moved back and forth like he was watching a movie, and I caught a reflection of something in his glasses. "Now it's the roofers opening the lid. Dr Card wants something in here, but they don't see anything… One guy says the word—rhodium." He looked up. "I'm sorry, that's all there is."

"Rhodium," Ellen said, giving me a knowing look.

But I was too distracted to listen to her. The mention of Dr. Card was a warning flare in my brain. I held out my hand to pull Roy out, and the silver lining mirrored our blurry reflections.

Suddenly the door flew open, and a bright flashlight swept our faces. "What are you doing here?" Niner strode through the door, a storm cloud forming on his face.

Roy yelped and jumped from the trunk.

"Is this another prank?" Niner demanded.

"No, sir," Roy said, but I cut him off.

"We remembered finding a copy of the patriot flag here in the attic, and we wanted to use it as a decoy."

"That's cheating," Niner said.

I snapped to attention in my best imitation of Jayden. "In war, it's strategy, sir."

Niner peered at me through narrowed eyes. "Back to the game."

I saluted and held my head high as I stalked from the room at the head of our crew. We marched solemnly down the stairs, but at the bottom I stopped. "Everyone spread out and hide around the house. Niner's up to something."

"I'll trail Niner," Ellen said.

"Everyone else, plant yourself in a room in case he goes there," I said.

I hid under Longfellow's desk in the library. Wide and solid, it felt like hiding in a cave. The grandfather clock on the stairs ticked softly, and the moonlight streaming through the window fell in patchwork squares across the books on the wall.

A shadowy form darted through the room. "Stella, where are you?"

"Under the desk," I whispered.

I heard a sigh, and Ellen squeezed in beside me. "It's happening. I'm getting a new sentence."

"Call Lindsey's name, and see if she answers."

Ellen took a deep breath, closed her eyes and tilted her chin toward the window. The beams from the full moon washed her face with light. Her eyes flew open. "She's there!" She was so excited she gave me a hug, and then let go and clutched her jaw. Even I could hear the buzz of her braces. "She didn't know her thoughts were going anywhere, but she says it must be the rhodium in the walls."

"Ask where she is," I said.

Ellen frowned. "She's a prisoner in a mine...with Dr. Card."

Prickles of fear ran down the back of my neck. "Where's the mine?" I asked.

"Near Philadelphia, on her uncle's farm."

"Get as much information as you can, and keep your connection. I'm going for the others."

I was so excited I didn't think straight, and I ran right into Niner walking through the trunk room.

"Ellen made contact with Lindsey! She's kidnapped by Dr. Card, and we need to rescue her—"

"I thought I told you to get back to the game," he said, turning me roughly by the shoulders.

TJ stood up from behind the trunk. "Ask Mr. Parker," she said. "He told Ellen to contact Lindsey."

Niner stared at us, his lip curling in a mean smile. "He isn't here. Called away on a *real* problem, not some kids imagining things."

I was so impatient my head buzzed like a hundred bees had gotten under my scalp. "Ellen wouldn't make up things like this."

Ellen and Roy arrived at that moment. "It's true," she said firmly, but Roy had picked up the tension in the room, and his eyes darted nervously from me to Niner.

"Fifty demerits from the Thornes, and you're all grounded," Niner barked. "Back to your dorm. Now."

None of us moved. Ellen stood as if in a trance. "She's locked in a room underground. The walls are crumbling, and she's afraid the next explosion will be the end."

I started for the door. "We're going to save her."

Niner sprang in front of me, holding my arm too tight. "No! I'm responsible for all of you." With a quick flick of his arm he pushed me into the attic and shut the door. I heard the lock click.

"Let her out," TJ cried.

"Everyone back to the dorm unless you want to be locked in, too," Niner roared.

I listened with hope that someone would get him to change his mind, but the only sounds were retreating footsteps and TJ's pleading growing fainter and fainter. Then a distant door slammed to a close, and I was alone.

I twisted the handle and kicked the door, but it wouldn't budge. If Jayden was here, he could unlock it. A creeping feeling of shame stole into my mind. I shouldn't have turned my back on him at the Capture-the-Flag game.

I sat down and ran my fingers over the grooves of the diagram cut in the floor. Every line met at the intersection of more lines—a confusing muddle. Like my mind trying to sort out our newest discoveries. The secret was in the lining, and it was rhodium! That's why Dr. Card sent the roofers. But why was he keeping Lindsey in a mine, and what did he want with rhodium?

I brought up an old image of Lindsey, dancing under the wind chimes on the tree at home—how was she now? Was she scared and lonely like me? I should have figured out she was missing sooner.

The moon slipped into view through the window at the far end of the attic. I stared at the bright disk, wishing that someone out there was thinking of me.

"Stella?"

It was Jayden's voice!

The lock clicked, and the door opened slowly. My first impulse was to burst out and hug him, but then I saw his frown.

"The others got me," he mumbled. He stepped back to reveal the anxious faces of my friends surrounding him.

"Thank you," I said, but the hardness in his face sent a pang through my heart. He didn't believe us.

He shrugged. "I'm going."

I ran after him, but he shook me off. "The others told me everything. You're out of control, Stella. You can't expect my help."

"Then why did you come and get me out?"

"Because you're still my friend."

My cheeks burned red, and frustration boiled up inside me. How could Jayden lecture me about doing what was right if he walked away now? I grabbed his arm. "If you're still my friend, then you need to believe me! Mr. Parker's gone, and there's no one else to rescue Lindsey."

Something flickered in Jayden's eyes. He might not believe all the stuff about the trunk and Dr. Card, but his first rule in life was doing the right thing, no matter the cost.

"Please," TJ said.

"Of course, he's coming," snapped Ellen. "How do we get there?"

I looked at Jayden. His eyes were still wary, but he nodded slowly.

I just hoped he'd listen to my plan. "We're going to teleport."

TJ let out a squeal of excitement, and Jayden studied my face as if sizing up whether I was serious.

I was serious—I just wasn't sure it would work.

ৼৡৡৡ

CHAPTER EIGHTEEN

ৼৡৡৡ

Ellen kept contact with Lindsey, and we figured out that by holding hands, I could get Lindsey's messages too.

She sent me the image of our destination—the dark mouth of a mine shaft cut in a rocky mountain. A wave of doubt rolled through my stomach. Were we crazy to rush off like this? But if we waited, we might be too late to save her.

"We need to leave a message for Mr. Parker," I said.

"I'll do it," Jayden said. "I'll meet you at the car."

He sprinted back to the game of Capture-the-Flag and re-joined us before we reached the garage behind Whittier House.

"Ivan's got the information," he reported. "He wanted to come with us, but I convinced him we need him here to pass on the message."

We piled into the old station wagon, with Roy, TJ, and Ellen in the back, and Jayden and me in the front. I took a deep breath to calm my nerves. The car smelled of wet carpet and stale french fries. I waited for everyone to fasten their seatbelts, and I thought I heard the sound of the rear door clicking open, but when I looked it was closed.

One last breath, and I inserted the key in the ignition. The others watched as I started the engine, their faces a mixture of curiosity and awe.

"Whoa," TJ murmured as I put the car in drive and let it roll forward.

The station wagon jounced over ruts in the dirt road, and I had a moment of terror trying to steer in the dark. Then Jayden reached over and flipped on the headlights.

"Thanks," I said.

The driving was easier after that. We made it to the main road, and I eased the car onto the smooth surface. "Everyone, hold on," I said. "We have to speed up for the tunnel."

I gunned the accelerator, and the car jerked forward, engine growling. My heart thumped painfully as we raced down the hill, faster and faster. I held the steering wheel steady, aiming for the middle of the opening. A second later the mouth of the tunnel swallowed us up, and the beam from the headlights disappeared.

The car hurtled forward into blackness, shaking violently. TJ and Roy screamed in the back seat, and I gripped the steering wheel so hard my fingers turned numb. I kept the image of the mine with its black opening and sharp rocks, and the roaring grew.

"Is this safe?" Jayden yelled.

"What next?" Ellen shouted.

"Watch for a light!"

My eyes ached with peering into the darkness ahead, and I started to worry. *What if this doesn't work? What if I get us killed?* A tight knot grew in my stomach, but just when I thought we couldn't hold on a moment longer, a point of light shone ahead, like a single candle in a black pit.

I swung the car toward it, and my hands seemed to know what to do—turning the steering wheel back and forth to follow the twisting passage. The light intensified until we shot out of the tunnel into the middle of a bunch of trailers with huge incandescent lights attached to the top.

I stomped on the brake, and the station wagon swerved inches from a brick shed and rattled to a stop beside it.

"Whoohoo!" Ellen shouted, looking behind us. "We came *out* of the mine."

I followed her gaze. Jagged rocks cast weird shadows around the black entrance.

A dog barked far away, and I suddenly felt exposed in the old station wagon under the glaring lights.

Where could we hide? I scanned the compound—lights blazed over every inch of the surrounding buildings. "We need to get in the mine," I said.

I twisted the handle on the door, but Roy laid a hand on my arm. "Wait. I'm getting a vision."

His glasses glinted back the reflection of the street lights. "It's people in strange clothes. Black triangle hats like Eugene wore in the play." He froze for a full minute, then shook himself as though waking up. "Paul Revere was here."

I knew the mine was old, but that was seriously old. "What did you see?"

"They were taking out cartloads of silver rocks."

"Rhodium," Ellen said in a breathless voice.

"Like the silver lining in the trunk," Jayden whispered. He glanced at me with new respect, and my heart squinched. Maybe I hadn't lost his friendship forever.

"We've got to move," Roy whispered. "I sense someone coming."

"Follow me." Jayden opened the door without making a sound and ran along the wall of the brick shed toward the mine. I kept low and scurried behind him, feeling like a mouse under the incandescent lights. From the shed we dashed for the mine entrance.

In the welcome darkness, I leaned against a bulging rock to catch my breath. The huddled shapes of the others briefly appeared as black forms against the light of the compound.

"We need to hold hands," I whispered.

I felt hands reaching for mine on both sides—Jayden in front, and a tiny hand that must have been TJ's behind. We shuffled forward. In the silence every pebble we kicked seemed to crash like thunder. Somewhere water dripped, and something vibrated softly beneath our feet.

We'd only gone about twenty steps when Ellen cried out as though she had been stung—three short yelps. "It's back—I can feel underground!" She sat down, bringing the whole line to the floor with her. She laughed and sobbed at the same time. "What a relief. . . I thought I'd lost it forever."

We didn't have time to celebrate. If we didn't get going, the guards would find us. "Ellen," I said firmly. "Concentrate—what is under us?"

She caught her breath, cutting off a last hiccupping laugh. "It's immense. Layers and layers of tunnel."

My heart plummeted like a rock in a mine shaft. We didn't have a chance in this labyrinth.

Ellen switched on her flashlight. "Lindsey says to go as deep as we can. It's safe to use a light now that we're away from the entrance. She's signing out because Dr. Card is coming back, but she'll try again in an hour."

"Can we still hold hands?" TJ asked in a hushed voice.

I gave her hand a squeeze. "Of course."

At that moment Ellen's flashlight flickered and went out. "Drat! Anyone else have a flashlight?"

"I forgot mine," Roy began, but TJ snapped on her own light.

"Anyone else?" I asked.

"It's the only one," Jayden said.

"It's okay," TJ announced. "I put in new batteries last week." She handed it to Ellen, who took Jayden's hand and stood for a moment, eyes closed. "The fastest way down goes to the left." She played the light over the passage. The walls were earth with rough rock jutting from them, stained green in splotches. With a shiver, I recognized the tunnel from my vision at camp.

Ellen pulled us ahead. We walked more quickly with the light to guide us, and I felt the clenching in my stomach begin to relax. At last we were on the right track.

Suddenly the vibration beneath our feet seemed to grow. Rocks and dirt showered down—sparkling like glitter. It stopped as quickly as it had begun, and Ellen held up a hand for us to pause. "The way is clear, but the mine doesn't feel steady. Are you sure you want to go on?"

"If Lindsey's down there, we need to try," Jayden said, and warm happiness bubbled up inside me. The old Jayden was back.

Ellen nodded and turned the flashlight on the shaft ahead. "We're going this way, but we've got a long way to go. It's best to save the light. I'll guide us by feel— hang on everyone." The light flicked off, and TJ gripped my hand harder.

Ellen narrated as we walked down the passage. "The ground is steeper here, and I'm slowing down. We've almost reached a bend." But after we turned the corner, her words seemed the same. Another steep slope, another turning, each one requiring caution. We maneuvered the fourth bend in the tunnel, and I began to wonder if we'd ever reach our goal.

My mind wandered to Lindsey. If only we'd figured out she was missing the first day. We had the strands of Longfellow poetry from Ellen and the wobbly vision of the earth-lined tunnel. I should have realized what was going on. Perhaps I was afraid to trust my gift.

I remembered Aunt Winnie's face when I didn't practice. She didn't trust me either. Slowly, a picture of Lindsey formed in my mind. She was swirling her dream catcher from her fingers and laughing. I held the picture, and suddenly the image blurred as though a slide show was on super fast-forward. I stumbled and would have fallen if Jayden hadn't held me up.

"Stop," he called.

I didn't know if he was talking to me or the group, but there was no stopping the flow of possibilities. They landed on an image of Lindsey, alone in a rocky cave. She sat on a packing case, stenciled with the words DANGER and HIGH EXPLOSIVE. I flinched.

Ellen switched on the flashlight, and the glow brought me back to the tunnel. Jayden had his hands on my shoulders. "You okay?"

"I saw Lindsey—she's alone, waiting for something."

Without warning, a thunderous boom filled the tunnel and the earth shuddered beneath our feet.

ᦒᦒ

CHAPTER NINETEEN

ᦒᦒ

I fell to the ground under a deluge of grit and gravel. The earthquake lasted so long I thought my bones had turned to jelly. My back was bruised from pelting rocks, and I tasted bitter dust in my mouth.

At last it stopped. The flashlight lay a few feet ahead of us, its beam lighting a swath of crumpled bodies and scattered stones. "Everyone okay?" My voice came out quavery and faint over the ringing in my ears.

One by one the others grunted or signaled.

Ellen's voice cut through the buzzing in my brain. "I don't think anyone can hear very well."

"Can you check if Lindsey's all right?"

She paused. "Nothing."

I was terrified that the explosion came from those boxes in Lindsey's cave. My bones ached, but terror sent me stumbling to my feet.

"We've got to get Lindsey." I shouted.

Ellen picked up the light. It wobbled in her hands and played on our faces—everyone covered in rubble and Roy with a red gash on his arm.

He wiped away the blood. "I'm okay."

The others brushed themselves off and tried to stand, tottering like a bunch of old people. My hearing began to return.

Ellen stood as still as a statue. "It's not safe." Her voice was raspy. "The tunnel could collapse anywhere."

We stared at each other. No one wanted to ask the question—did we dare go on?

"How close are we?" I asked.

She pointed the flashlight at our feet. "She's directly below us."

"We can't go back now," TJ said.

I looked at the others, and they all nodded. Without a word we took hands again. A current of resolve seemed to travel from hand to hand. Jayden tugged me ahead, and I pulled on TJ.

"Corner," Ellen sang out, and there was a note of determination that hadn't been there before. I rounded the bend, and far down the tunnel stood a wooden door. We dropped hands and ran, TJ whooping and calling Lindsey's name. Jayden arrived first and tried the handle, which didn't budge.

"Lindsey!" He pounded on the door.

"She's locked in…" Ellen began but was interrupted by a triumphant grunt from Jayden, who released the lock. The door swung open on a dimly lit room.

Lindsey ran forward, trying to hug all of us at once. Her blonde hair was braided and wound around her head, and the rock dust sparkled in it. "I knew you'd come," she said.

Ellen stood off to the side, slowly turning in a circle. "We've got to get out of here. These walls aren't stable."

Lindsey ran to a pile of stones and dirt in the corner and began pushing away the larger rocks. "We have to get Dr. Card first. He's trapped in a tunnel."

I thought she'd gone insane—deep in the mine, locked in a room with walls collapsing.

"What are you talking about?" I said. "He's not our problem."

Jayden was watching me intently, but I stared him down. "We can't do anything," I said. "We'll barely make it out ourselves."

"There's always something we can do," he said quietly.

I felt the piece of rope in my pocket and remembered the vision of my parents promising Ethan Card they would do all they could. I remembered how the boy threw back his head to wail their loss, and I realized I couldn't leave Dr. Card if there was a chance he was alive.

I had to carry out the promise my parents didn't live to keep.

Clenching my hand around the rope, I concentrated on Lindsey scrabbling at the pile of rubble and willed the possibilities to come. My head ached and a roaring filled my brain, but the possibilities slowly advanced until I knew what to do.

"Jayden—can you move these rocks?"

He stepped forward and raised his arms, and a mound rolled away from the corner like a wave of the sea—a gray mass flecked with sparkling bits, lifting and surging. The first wave crested in the middle of the room, and a second wave followed. Sweat trickled down his forehead, but he kept working.

Lindsey backed away and watched him tensely. "There's more to Dr. Card."

"I know," I said. I pulled out the rope, and her face grew pale.

"Is that—"

But I never heard what she was going to say. As though a dam had broken, images flooded my mind. I saw Dr. Card as I had seen him last—grabbing the Pandora Device. Then he was standing in a cemetery, head bowed.

The torrent of possibilities streamed past—Dr. Card working feverishly over notes in a laboratory, adjusting a machine, swirling a silver substance in a test tube. With each image his face changed, the ruthlessness seemed to drain away and was replaced with a deep sorrow. In the last image he bent over a lab table, utterly defeated, holding in his hands a coil of rope.

I suddenly understood what drove him. He wanted to save his mother.

"I need some light," Jayden called. The mound in the center of the room had grown so high I couldn't see him. We ran to the corner, where only his sneakers stuck out of a hole.

I held the flashlight inside and gasped. Dr. Card lay unconscious, his legs pinned under the rocks of a collapsed tunnel. Jayden rubbed the surface and pieces of gravel sifted out, pooling on the ground. "It's worse than I thought," he said. "I have to pull him out. Everyone back."

An edge in his voice sent me scooting to the far wall. The next moment a sound like rock grating on rock filled the room. Jayden yelled, a weird desperate yell, and the ceiling seemed to lift up for a moment then settle down with a crash. Dirt rained on our heads, and Jayden's body flew from the hole, followed by the limp form of Dr. Card, whose hands he held.

They hit the wall, and Jayden moaned. Dr. Card lay eerily still. I rushed to help Jayden, but he waved me off. "I'm fine—help him."

Ellen pressed her fingers against Dr. Card's wrist, her voice shrill. "I don't feel a pulse."

"His brain is still alive. I can feel his thoughts," Lindsey said.

I closed my eyes and concentrated on the possibilities again. Before I even took a breath, they came rolling through my brain. My mind felt light, the summoning effortless. "TJ needs to touch him."

She timidly came forward and reached out her hand, and before she even made contact, an electric spark flew between them.

Dr. Card opened his eyes. He coughed, and his breath came in ragged gasps. Then, he pushed himself up, and his glance darted around the cavern with a haunted expression.

"We have to get out!" he said.

Jayden helped him to his feet, but a rumbling grew from the direction of the passageway. I braced for another deluge of rocks, but the tremor quickly subsided.

Ellen pressed her hand against the door, and her eyes flew wide in panic. "The tunnel's gone."

Dr. Card groaned and stared at the ground. "You should have left me," he said, his voice flat.

"We saw a different possibility," I said.

His head jerked up. "You? Here?"

I waited for the next possibility to come, but the flood had run dry. Jayden looked at me, his face a question, but I shook my head. "We have to wait for the next possibility," I said.

I just hoped there was one.

We sat in silence. Jayden extinguished one of the lanterns, and I knew he was conserving the air in the cave.

In the semi-darkness Dr. Card turned to me. "I'm sorry for what happened to your parents."

His words should have made me feel better, but I felt flat, as though the possibilities had consumed my emotions and only the barest residue was left. "I don't believe you," I said.

His shoulders sagged. "I wish I could do things over. Your parents were different. They never gave up, even if it cost them to do what was right."

The cost of doing what was right. I'd been paying it all my life. It hurt to think about my parents, but perhaps now I was beginning to understand. I closed my eyes and searched for a possibility again, and I saw something amazing. "Roy, can you connect to the past here?"

Roy had been sitting with his head on his knees, but he looked up. "I'll try."

I watched him, hoping my possibilities were right.

"I'm getting a vision," he cried at last.

"Everyone, hold hands so we can see it," I said.

Our team moved as one, joining hands in a chain, with TJ on the end by Dr. Card.

The clopping of horses' hooves drew my eyes to a section of wall where the rock jutted out like a ship. A shadowy figure on a horse came through the stone, which parted before him.

Beside me Ellen gasped. "Did you see that—right through the stone!"

My senses seemed suddenly more acute, as though the air itself was vibrating with sensations—the smell of the horse, the creak of the saddle, the sparkle of light on the silver stirrups.

The man wore a black tricorn hat and knee breeches and carried a lantern. "I have come for thee," he said. With a shock I realized he was speaking directly to us.

"There's no way out," Roy replied.

The man laughed a hearty laugh, and it made my skin tingle like a splash of cold water on a hot morning. "For the kin of Temperance Card, there is always a way from the Townsend Mine."

Dr. Card stared at the man in wonder. "You know my mother?"

The Revere Factor

"I know Temperance Card, but she is not thy mother. She searches for thee." He swept off his hat, and the silver buckle on the brim glistened. "Paul Revere at thy service."

Dr. Card paled and tried to speak, but his voice came out as a croak. "The year. What year is it?"

"The year of our Lord, 1776"

"Eighty-four years later," Dr. Card muttered. "How can that be?"

Revere held his lantern higher, casting a glow on his square chin and wide-spaced eyes. He seemed to be looking beyond us as he spoke. "I link across time to bring thee a message from Temperance Jerusha Card— the fate of the nation is in thy hands. Thou must return to thy time."

Dr. Card's glance flicked toward me. "There is no known device for time travel."

"There is a trunk that must be found."

I looked at Roy, who was grinning. He must have recognized the trunk too. "We know where it is," I said.

Revere bowed in my direction. "It will transport him. You have the rope still?"

"He does," I said. I broke the chain for a moment to pass it to Dr. Card.

He held the rope in his shaking hand and groaned, deep and sorrowful. "All my work has been futile."

"No," Revere said. "It has brought thee to this moment. Now thou must follow me at once." He looked at Roy and saluted. "Thou dost not need to maintain the vision for the others. The properties of this mine give every man the power to see for himself."

He turned his horse and disappeared through the wall, which closed behind him like a curtain.

Ellen ran to the spot. "It's a secret door."

Jayden joined her, running his hands over the rough surface, and slowly a section of rock swung inward onto a tall, narrow passage.

Dr. Card rose on shaky legs. He was only a little taller than me, and despite the layer of dust, I could see that his hair had turned completely white since I saw him last.

Revere waited for us astride his horse on the other side of the door. "I must talk with Ethan Card," he said.

Dr. Card limped forward eagerly, like a shipwrecked man who has seen a life boat.

They led the way through the passage, which wound gradually upward. Revere leaned over the horse to speak quietly to Dr. Card, and he simply listened. He began the long hike with bent back and hesitant steps, but as he walked beside Revere, he grew taller and straighter. A faint light glowed around them, and the face he turned to us at the end of the tunnel had lost the deep frown lines.

Revere clucked to his horse and rode away. Dr. Card stood frozen, watching him.

TJ took his hand, but her touch did not spark this time. "Are you all right?"

He was still clutching the piece of rope and he looked down at it, speaking softly. "Revere says I must return to my own time, but I cannot save my mother. It will be too late—I can only return to the year I would have lived at my current age." He shook his head. "So many lost years." His eyes locked with mine. "What is done cannot be undone."

"What will you do?" I asked.

"He cannot tell me my mission, but he assures me I will recognize it. Revere says there is something I need from you before I can go."

His words sent the blood pounding in my ears.

Dr. Card's penetrating gaze rested on me. "I'm sorry," he said. "For all the harm I've caused you." The grief in his eyes seemed to numb my brain.

I tried to speak, but the words caught in my throat. From the moment I first saw him as a child with my parents, I had known what I needed to do. But it was too hard. For too long I had dreamed of striking back at Dr. Card—making him suffer the way I had.

When you want something badly enough, it burns and churns and gnaws in you. I thought I'd prove myself by getting revenge on Dr. Card for my parents' deaths, but what I realized now was that proving myself didn't mean getting what I wanted—it meant doing what I didn't want. For me, that was the hardest thing of all—forgiveness.

Dr. Card turned away. "It's wrong for me to ask this of you."

Suddenly the thread of possibilities spun out like a spool unwinding. I saw myself turning my back on Dr. Card, bitterness on my face. The next frames repeated the scene, only this time with Ellen, then TJ, then Jayden, then Lindsey, until I was alone. My face had changed—it was hard and angry. A series of images followed, and they scared me. I was doing terrible things but my eyes gleamed viciously. "No!" I cried. I refused to see any more.

I opened my eyes and focused on Dr. Card, and the old ache for my parents came rushing back. It seemed like the two of us were locked in a cycle of pain—hating and grieving until the wound got worse and worse. There was only one way out.

My voice choked on the words, but I managed to say them clearly. "I forgive you."

He bowed his head.

"Well done," came faintly from the tunnel end. Revere was gone, and the pale yellow of dawn glowed from the entrance.

I began to run toward it, but Dr. Card darted forward and caught my arm. For a moment I thought he'd changed back to the ruthless scientist I'd known, but his face was twisting with a different emotion—fear. "The international director is overseeing operations. He mustn't see us."

"We have a car," I began.

"Where?"

"Behind the brick shed."

He crept to the entrance and scanned the compound. "Follow me." He ran toward the shed and darted inside with us close behind him.

Inside, three huge black contraptions squatted against one wall. They looked like giant cannonballs that someone hollowed out and decorated with a funnel for a mouth. Black pipes rose above them, and white tendrils of smoke leaked from the nearest one. TJ leaned against it and jumped back. "It's warm."

Dr. Card rubbed a dirt-blackened arm across his eyes. "We've been trying to separate rhodium all week in these smelters, but the process isn't working."

A hissing sound startled us, but it was just one of the smelters belching a cloud of steam.

"Be careful where you step," Dr. Card whispered. "They didn't rake up the coals from the fire. We've got to reach the car."

"Why the car?" asked a deep voice.

Dr. Card turned white and spun toward the sound. "Director, I'm just sending back some interns to Camp Hawthorne. They were on a field trip…"

"Remember, I can see through lies," the man interrupted. "I missed you at the morning conference."

"There was an accident in the mines."

"Clearly." The director motioned to a gang of men who stepped from the shadows. "You know what to do."

I felt a sweet-smelling cloth pressed against my nose, and the room went black.

❧❧❧

CHAPTER TWENTY

❧❧❧

I woke up in the back of the old station wagon with Jayden and Lindsey on either side of me. Another body dropped next to us—Ellen. I pretended to be unconscious until the door snapped shut. "Anyone awake?" I whispered.

From the front seat TJ's small voice came. "I'm here, and Niner, too."

"Niner? What's he doing here?"

"I don't know—I can't wake him." TJ stopped as the side door opened and another body was dumped on the seat. The door slammed close.

"Everyone's here," TJ whispered.

I heard the sound of someone settling into the front seat, a grunt, and the car started.

I wished Lindsey would wake up. She could make a mental connection between all of us. I called into her mind, but no answer.

I tried to raise my head but dizziness took over, and I passed out again. I woke up the second time when the car stopped with a lurch. The driver jumped out, and I had a quick glimpse of his leering face through the back window. He pushed the car, and it rolled forward slowly, then began to pick up speed.

"We're on a steep hill," TJ quavered.

I forced myself to sit up, the world spinning. "Can you get in the driver's seat?"

She crawled sideways, but the car bounced over a rut, sending us in the air. In that moment the road in front of us clicked into focus. We were barreling down an old dirt track that ran along a cliff. The sight sent a shock that cleared the last of the haze from my brain.

"Push the brake," I yelled.

"I'm pushing, but it's not working!"

The trees flew past. I scrambled over the unconscious Niner and squeezed into the passenger seat. There should have been an emergency brake, but it wasn't in the middle like I expected. The car sped faster, and my stomach turned to stone.

TJ whimpered. The road curved ahead. If we didn't make the turn, we'd go sailing over the edge.

The image of the station wagon flying over the cliff flashed in my head. Someone behind me was screaming, and my thoughts froze. Then I reached out for the possibilities. I knew I could do it now. . . My throat tightened and I braced myself, pushing against the picture of the flying car in my mind. It slid back to the image of a foot pushing a brake.

"The black pedal by the door—stomp on it!" I yelled.

TJ jammed her foot, hugging the steering wheel for support. The station wagon jerked and skidded sideways, and my body slammed into the door. With a metallic crash, we smashed into a huge pine tree and stopped.

I groaned and slowly crawled out of the car. The others must have woken up during our wild ride, and they climbed out after me. Ellen had a scrape across her cheek, and Dr. Card shuffled a few steps and sat down.

Niner was the last to rouse. "What's going on?" he demanded.

"It's not a prank," TJ said.

He rubbed a bleeding gash on his forehead. "I know—I hid in the car. Thought I'd save you from your crazy scheme, but the guard found me." He squinted at the group—our faces streaked with grime—and his gaze fell on Dr. Card. "Who are you?"

"Ethan Card."

Niner staggered to his feet and in one swift movement pulled Dr. Card to his feet and pinned his arm behind him. "It is my duty to arrest you on behalf of the SBI." The effort made his voice crack.

"He's not the one you want," TJ shouted, throwing her body between them so that Niner let go. "He's got to save America and everything else!" She spread her arms in front of Dr. Card.

Niner straightened. His strength was rapidly returning, and he could probably have lifted both of them over his shoulder like two sacks, but he stepped back and looked at me. "Is this true?"

I nodded, and Niner sat back down in the front seat of the car. He dropped his head into his hands. "I should've listened earlier." He looked down the road, where the rising sun glinted off the gray rocks that lined the cliff, and he shuddered. "Someone was trying to kill us. We need to get out of here before they realize it didn't work."

"How do we do that?" TJ asked.

"Stella's going to take us back to camp," he said.

My stomach spiraled. "But the brakes aren't working."

He chuckled grimly. "I'll be right beside you, and we'll use speed to our advantage. We'll aim for the tunnel at the bottom there."

I looked where he pointed. The road curved around and disappeared into a narrow hole cut in the mountain. I tried to take a relaxing breath, but my lungs had quit working.

Niner set his jaw. "The thing to remember is to steer away from the cliff. Everyone be ready if I tell you to lean to the right."

My legs were shaking as I returned to the car. I wiped sweaty hands on my jeans and took hold of the steering wheel.

In the rearview mirror, TJ's face was white and determined. "Let's go," she said.

The engine sputtered to life, and with it came a sour gasoline smell.

"Let up on the accelerator," Niner said. "I'll help you steer. You've got the image of camp?"

I nodded, my mouth too dry to talk. If we didn't make it to the tunnel, what would happen?

The station wagon rolled down the hill, huffing louder as it gained speed.

Niner held the steering wheel with iron strength and kept us from veering off the edge of the cliff, while everyone leaned to the side to help us turn. The tunnel was narrow, more like a mine shaft. At the last minute Niner wrenched the wheel to the side. The front bumper tore away with a crash, but the rest of the car made it.

We rocketed through the tunnel, and he let go, roaring his final instructions over the noise of teleportation. "It's up to you now—picture the road at Camp Hawthorne."

I concentrated so hard that stars exploded in front of my eyes, blurring at last with the circle of light at the mouth of the tunnel.

"You did it," Jayden yelled.

We burst from the tunnel, and I drove up the hill toward the camp entrance, but the car sputtered and the steering wheel froze. Niner started laughing as the car drifted to a stop. "I guess you forgot to check the gas before you left."

We walked the rest of the way to Longfellow House, though Dr. Card would probably have run if he could. A strange light gleamed in his eyes, and he strode ahead as though the trunk in the attic was drawing him. TJ jogged at his side, humming the "Listen" song.

"Are there words to that song?" he asked.

She began singing softly. After the first chorus, he joined in, his deep voice blending with her high clear notes. "Listen, listen, listen for me." In the early morning hush, it seemed that even the birds stopped singing to listen.

No one was awake when we arrived, and Niner led the way up the stairs to the piles of boxes outside the attic.

Dr. Card caught sight of the diagram in the floor first. It glowed in a patch of sunlight, and he bent down to run long, delicate fingers over the lines.

"This is the spy network used during the Revolutionary War," he said. "I'd heard rumors of it, but I've never seen it for myself. You can read the initials—PR for Paul Revere, RT for Robert Townsend, and someone named 355. I wonder. . ." He stared at the three numbers as if they could answer his question.

TJ sat next to him. "They used rhodium, didn't they?"

"Yes—though they didn't know it was rhodium then. They called it the *Revere factor*. Paul Revere discovered that the ore from the Townsend Mine enhanced mental conductivity, and he used it for the network. Brilliant."

He drew a finger along one of the lines. "These lines connected the ESP practitioners with others who could receive their messages. They didn't have the gift, but the rhodium enabled them to receive transmissions. They hid the metal in buttons, stirrups, even the Liberty Bell. Revere's trunk was the center."

I thought of the vast network of spies who helped the American patriots, and I felt the familiar tingle of possibilities. Was Dr. Card linked to them in some way? Is that why Revere said he must go back?

Dr. Card walked to the trunk and rested his hands on the scarred wooden lid. "The roofers reported nothing here, but they didn't recognize the lining."

He opened the lid, and the silver coating sparkled around him. "Almost pure rhodium. I created a theory with rhodium as a connector, but I never thought I'd live to see it." His face broke into a radiant smile. "And now I know it works!"

He turned to TJ. "I'm going back with a new purpose, my dear."

"I'm sorry you can't see your mother," she said quietly.

Dr. Card put his hand on her shoulder. "No, but there will be another Temperance Jerusha."

She raised her chin. "There's been one in the family in every generation."

I looked from one to the other, and the truth hit me. TJ was Temperance Jerusha—named for Dr. Card's mother.

Dr. Card appeared taller than he had before. He pulled out the rope and stepped into the trunk. "I'll leave a message for you at the Junction Stone," he said.

TJ ran forward and hugged him hard. He bowed his head over her, and the reflection in the trunk lining shimmered and changed. The taller figure wore a tricorn hat, and the girl wore a dress with a square collar.

I looked at Roy, and his eyes grew wide. "Did you see it too?"

"I thought it was a possibility…" I began.

"But it's also the past," he said.

Dr. Card, smiling confidently, reached up and closed the lid.

A low roar built around us, and a thin streak of white glowed at the edges of the trunk. Instinctively, I reached for TJ's hand, and saw that everyone else was linked in a semi-circle in front of the trunk. A final clap of thunder extinguished the light, leaving us in deep silence. The lid smoked slightly. "Is he all right?" TJ whispered.

Jayden touched the lock, and the lid flew open. There was nothing inside but the silver lining.

❧❧

CHAPTER TWENTY-ONE

❧❧

Mr. Parker returned at lunch, his green bow tie askew and dust in his hair, but a wide smile for all of us. Ivan had passed on our message, and the SBI moved in quickly.

"It was abandoned by the time we got there," Mr. Parker said. "But we took possession of the mine and all the rhodium ore."

We filled in the rest of the details for him, and he shook his head thoughtfully throughout the account. "I agree that Ethan Card should have gone back," he said. "Though I'm not sure the SBI would have been able to approve the transport so quickly." His eyes gleamed with a hint of mischief.

"I wanted to ask you about the spark that TJ gave Dr. Card," I said. "Does she have a healing gift?"

Mr. Parker shook his head wonderingly. "I never thought it was possible, but from what you tell me, it was a life spark that she could give because she was descended from him."

"What about the trunk—could it be used for time travel?" Jayden asked.

"Not unless every molecule in your body was meant for another time period. Rhodium enhances the powers that draw a displaced person to the time where he belongs. The rope must have helped as well. But rhodium has lots of other uses."

"Like a communication network?" Jayden asked.

"I'm sure the SBI will be studying the possibility."

Though Lindsey made it through the mine rescue, she collapsed from exhaustion the morning we got back to camp. She had to stay in the infirmary the rest of the week. Ivan was so attentive, he seemed more like a genie in a bottle than a nurse. He brought her books and fruit, and roasted s'mores for her with fire from his fingertips.

Ellen helped us find the message from Dr. Card at the Junction Stone. Her powers returned at the mine, and she suspected it was due to the action of rhodium. She had filled her pockets with rocks before we left.

"There are only specks in the rocks," she explained. "But I showed Mr. Parker, and he says I can ask the orthodontist to add a piece of wire made from rhodium to counteract the effect from the braces."

The rocks in her pockets worked fine. She brushed against the Junction Stone and her face lit up. "There's rhodium here, too! See the sparkles in the stone?"

She walked around it twice and pointed to a spot a little to the side where we should dig.

Niner joined us at this point, and with a shock I realized I was seeing the scene that had flashed in my mind days ago: Jayden and Niner digging at the Junction Stone, and Ellen and me joining them. With the four of us working, the hole grew rapidly.

At last a rusty box appeared. TJ opened it and pulled out a square item wrapped in a cloth. She barely breathed as she peeled back the layers. Inside lay a tiny book. Carefully she opened the cover, and her eyes welled with tears. "To TJ," she read in a whisper.

She handed the book to me, and I read the rest for her. Only the first two pages contained words.

My dear, I have lived a full life, and now I am old. Though the damage I have done cannot be undone, I have strived to set things right in the time I have left. I have lived to see my son's daughter, the second Temperance Jerusha, grow into a young woman. I have taught her all I know, and she will lead the spies during the Revolutionary War. Her code name will be 355, and she will use the song you taught me as her watchword. When you sing it, remember me.

I can retire now knowing that all is safe. The pioneering work of my granddaughter will lead to the foundation of the SBI. In her old age she will teach a young man named Nathaniel Hawthorne to use his gift.

The rest of this book is left for you to finish, my dear. Remember always—forgiveness and new life.

With deep love and affection,
  Ethan Card

We were quiet for a long time after that. TJ held the book cupped in her hands while tears fell softly on the cloth wrapping.

≈≈

Chapter Twenty-Two

≈≈

After TJ's discovery, I needed to be quiet for a while. I took the path to the lake, feeling oddly empty after all the excitement.

"Do you have a minute to talk?" Jayden caught up with me and motioned to a fallen log beside the trail. I sat beside him, the branches rustling overhead and leaf shadows shifting around us.

"Is Niner lurking around?" I was only half-joking.

"It's not what you think." Jayden scowled. "Only a few of us knew it, but the SBI sent him to camp because they picked up on a threat."

"Why didn't you tell me?"

"I had to keep the secret." He raised one eyebrow. "I *do* believe in following rules, you know."

I laughed. Jayden was right—I was always thinking that certain rules didn't apply to friends, and that's where Niner and I fell out.

"Niner regrets he didn't trust you earlier," he said.

"It's okay. I didn't trust him either." Until I said the words, I didn't realize I was as much to blame as Niner.

I stared out at the woods, tree after tree spreading as far as I could see. Sometimes I got an ache in my gut from wishing so hard I could *do* something to make a difference the way my parents did. But this summer I learned that sometimes you make a difference not by doing, but by letting go. When I forgave Dr. Card, I let go of the bitterness against him, and I felt new.

"In the mine I thought Lindsey was insane," I said. "I couldn't understand why she'd risk all our lives, insisting we save Dr. Card. But she taught me something. There's an incredible power in forgiveness."

"So you forgive me?" Jayden asked.

"For what—trying to keep me out of fights with Joanne?"

"I thought you were out of control."

"I guess in a way I was. I'm sorry too."

"You did the right thing." He held out a hand. "Friends?" he said.

"Friends." He kept hold of my hand, and we walked down to the lake together.

For the rest of camp I spent every afternoon with Lindsey in the infirmary, talking about what happened. For some reason both of us needed it—she to talk and me to listen.

"The mine has been in our family for generations," she told me. "I picked up from my great uncle that something was seriously wrong, and that's why I wrote to you. Later, I learned his heart attack was caused by the pressure from the Human Project to sell the mine."

I listened as Lindsey explained how she came to be trapped in the mine. Dr. Card knew her family was leaving—Lindsey for camp and the rest of her family for a Florida vacation. Her great uncle would be homebound for a while. Dr. Card planned to secretly take over the mine for two weeks to extract as much rhodium as possible. In preparation, he monitored the mail, and that's why my letter was returned.

When Dr. Card moved onto the property, he didn't realize Lindsey was still there. She was staying with her great uncle until the bus picked her up, and she stumbled on his operation. He had to keep her quiet.

"Were you scared?" I asked.

Lindsey smiled, her eyes wide with her far-away look. "I was treated well, even though I was locked in a cell inside the mine. Dr. Card brought old records, which he let me study. We both wanted to figure out what gave the mine its special properties, and during the hours poring over old documents we somehow became friends."

She told me about his years at Harvard and how he made important breakthroughs in physics. He joined the Human Project because he thought their research would help him save his mother.

He was absolutely driven by one idea—travelling back in time to save her. It blinded him to the evil methods used by the Human Project, and he became as ruthless as the director.

"But he wasn't ruthless with me," she said. "He sent the message to camp that I would be delayed, and he planned to be gone before anyone figured out what was going on. Unfortunately, extracting rhodium from the ore was more difficult than he anticipated. Then the international director came to oversee things himself, and everything went wrong after that.

"The director didn't like that I knew so much," she explained. "And Dr. Card thought my life was in danger. He was helping me escape when the mine collapsed. It had grown unstable from too much blasting in the rock. I'm glad you came when you did."

Lindsey hoped to help with rhodium research at the SBI someday. She believed it had healing properties based on the way Dr. Card changed during the week in the mine. But I wondered if Lindsey had more to do with it than the rhodium. Nevertheless, Ellen shared the rocks with her. She kept them in a bag by her bed, and she did seem to get better every day.

Since Lindsey had finally arrived at camp, the CITs decided to give a special repeat performance of *The Midnight Ride of Paul Revere*.

They brought her in a wheelchair to the barn at Alcott House, where she watched the show from the front row. During the closing lines, the image of Paul Revere returned to my mind, and I looked at Lindsey whose eyes were glowing.

For, borne on the night-wind of the Past,
Through all our history, to the last,
In the hour of darkness and peril and need,
The people will waken and listen to hear
The hurrying hoof-beats of that steed,
And the midnight message of Paul Revere.

꽃꽃

CHAPTER TWENTY-THREE

꽃꽃

The last days of camp flew by. We had the annual band performance given by the telekinetics. Jayden played the flute, and TJ clapped so hard for his solo that I thought she was going to self-combust. The Whits won the robotics competition with a huge green leaf-shaped robot inspired by the middle name of their hero, John *Greenleaf* Whittier. We had campfires and canoeing and swimming in the lake.

Niner invited our team to attend a last meeting with Mr. Parker. He called it a "debriefing." I didn't mind the strange lingo now that I knew he was from the SBI.

He wore a suit and carried a briefcase full of papers, which he shuffled around for a couple minutes.

"There are a few items to wrap up," he began. "First, we learned that the roofers planted the mp3 player to aid their return to Camp Hawthorne. We used it to trace the Human Project to one of their strategic bases, and we arrested several members. We're getting closer to shutting down the entire operation."

He turned to me. "I want to personally thank Stella for her part in this."

"I'm sorry I broke your rules," I said.

He winked. "It's called strategy in time of war."

"And the Revere trunk?" Mr. Parker asked.

"It's at the lab, and we've already harnessed some remarkable properties as a communication link. This information is classified, and I will rely on all of you to keep it a secret."

He closed his brief case with a snap. "There is one last duty I have." He scanned the room—Jayden, Ellen, Lindsey and me. "For reasons that will become clear, the SBI thought it best for your families to know the nature of this camp and your training here. One of you has an operative in your family already," he added. "But that's classified information and you will only be told if it is mission-critical."

I was so surprised I breathed in too fast and a choking sound came out. "We can tell our families everything?"

"Everything."

If I was a telekinetic like Jayden, I would have been floating around the room. Instead, I savored the image of Grandma in her recliner with me telling her all about camp and the gifts I'd found there.

Niner shook Jayden firmly by the hand. "Good job, sergeant," he said.

He shook my hand as well. "If you ever have an interest in enemy subversion, look me up. I have a feeling you were made for it."

I told him good-bye and was tempted to add "see you around," but then maybe that wasn't possible. With his talent for camouflage, he only let us see him when he wanted.

After he left, I asked Jayden what *subversion* meant. He didn't know either, so we looked it up in the dictionary at the Twain House library. The entry read:

Subversion refers to an attempt to transform the established social order and its structures of power, authority, and hierarchy.

I wondered if subversion might be another gift.

Before I was ready, the final day came. At dinner, the new canoe paddle was hung in the dining hall in honor of Niner and Skeeter, and the ceremonial closing campfire followed.

Ivan kicked off the evening by throwing a fire ball to light the pile of sticks. We sang all the usual songs, ending with our new one.

Listen, listen, listen for me.

The soft notes floated on the air, and I imagined the song passing through time from the days of the American patriots to all the kids who ever came to Camp Hawthorne.

At last Mr. Parker stood up to award the silver trophy to the team with the most points. I caught the glum expression on Eugene's face. Even his gung-ho spirit couldn't overcome the hundreds of demerits we'd gotten. It was depressingly true that "what was done could not be undone." Mr. Parker began by praising the Alcotts who had quietly accumulated points by doing good deeds around camp. In addition, they had kept the prison so well for Capture-the-Flag, that our team won the war through sheer attrition. No one who went into prison ever came out!

Mr. Parker continued. "There are, however, some additional points to award tonight. The staff voted unanimously to award two hundred points for the successful rescue of our fellow camper, Lindsey Townsend, which brings the Thornes to a tie with the worthy Alcotts. Well done, everyone!"

The CITs from both dorms came forward to receive the trophy. Eugene punched his fist to the sky in a victory salute, and everyone cheered, the Thornes loudest of all.

The next morning, Aunt Winnie arrived in her wheelchair at breakfast to say good-bye. I'd learned a lot with her during our last few days, and she was her usual energetic self again.

"Keep practicing," she told me. "I'll expect a letter from you every month to report on your progress."

"I promise to work harder," I said. And this time I knew I could do it.

After breakfast I walked to the dorm to get my suitcase and found myself alone with Joanne. She stood in the middle of the room, frowning and twisting the handle of her duffle bag back and forth.

"Can we talk?" she muttered.

I glanced at her quickly, ready to run or duck if this was another prank.

"I'm sorry for everything," she blurted. "It's nothing personal—I just don't like little kids."

"I know." We both started laughing. The new contrite version of Joanne set me off, and I guess it was a relief for her to actually talk.

She turned to leave, and I almost missed my chance. "Hey," I called. "I'm sorry I accused you of bringing the mp3 player."

"That's okay," she said, a goofy smile spreading on her face. "But you thought it was real music, right?"

I may not have liked it, but it was certainly real music. "Yeah—real music. Where did it come from?"

"It's another gift I have," she said shyly. "I can make music out of thin air, but my parents don't approve. They don't want me to tell anyone about it." She frowned and kicked the bunk bed. "But I'm going to start a band and be a rock star someday."

"I believe you."

"You do?"

And for the first time I realized there was a real person inside Joanne. I shut my eyes and willed the possibilities to come. Sharp and clear, images of Joanne flipped past, one after the other. Joanne in a garage with a guy and some drums. A coffee shop with Joanne at a microphone and some musicians behind her, and finally a huge auditorium with fans waving their arms and Joanne and her band on the stage. I opened my eyes again. "You're going to do it," I said.

Joanne gave me a ferocious hug and dashed off to catch her bus.

I packed the last of my clothes and joined the others to say good-bye to Ivan's team.

"You gotta visit," Ivan said. "Any chance your team could join a 4-H club? We're going to a conference in the fall, and we could meet you there."

"Do they have horses?" Lindsey asked.

"Of course."

"We'll be there."

Their bus pulled away, and Ivan waved with his arms stuck out the windows and his fingers trailing black smoke and fire until they turned a corner out of sight.

Our bus was the last to leave, and Mr. Parker shook each of our hands before we stepped on board. Sarah stood beside him and slipped me a small blue volume. "Longfellow's poetry," she said. "I wrote one of his quotes in the front for you."

The bus rattled down the dirt track toward the highway, and someone started the camp song. I let the rowdy singing swirl around me while I retreated into my own cocoon, keeping a picture of Sarah in a flowing print dress bright in my mind. I opened the book slowly. Her handwriting was a work of art in itself. In bold flourishes she had penned:

If we knew the secret history of our enemies, we would find sorrow and suffering enough to disarm all hostility."
~Henry Wadsworth Longfellow in *"Driftwood"*

We passed under the Camp Hawthorne sign, swaying gently from the log arch. I thought of all that had happened this summer. The most extraordinary power I witnessed at camp this year had come unexpectedly—the power of forgiveness.

The bus raced through the tunnel, and the teleportation energy surged through me—the blackness, the roaring sounds, the shaking speed. I peered ahead, searching for the pinpoint of light, which grew and grew until we burst into the sunlight. We were home.

Grandma was waiting for me at the school, along with all the other families. She folded me in a hug and held on tight. I had so much to tell her I didn't know where to start.

At home she had my favorite gingersnaps waiting on a plate in the living room, and we settled into chairs. "I want to hear everything," she said. "But first I have a little gift for you. I made some extra money doing a job for a friend, and I thought you might like this."

She handed me a tiny red box. Inside was a delicate silver ring with a sparkling blue stone shaped like a teardrop. "It's your birthstone—aquamarine. And the sterling silver is finished with rhodium."

"Rhodium?"

Grandma's face crinkled in a smile. "Now tell me about your camp."

ABOUT THE AUTHOR

Joyce McPherson is the author of books for young people as well as a director for Shakespearean theatre. She is also the mother of nine children, who give useful advice for her stories. She has never been to Camp Hawthorne, but still hopes for an invitation someday.

ACKNOWLEDGMENTS

Thank you to the moon and back to all the teachers, librarians, and bookstore wonders who have placed a copy of this book into the hands of a young person. And to all the bloggers who have spread the word, and to all the fans who have shared your enthusiasm with me and others, THANK YOU! I would thank you all by name if I could!

A special thank you to Garth, Heather, Alexie, Duncan, Andrew, David M., Grace, Connor, Luke, Emily, Laurie, Sally, Cathy, Marilyn, Laura, Kashmira, David Y., Meg, Tanya W., Jonathan, Elena, Kat, Lauren, Alexis, Catherine, Rachael, Lindsey, Mira, Jenn, Mary, Maria Luisa, Jenifer, Taylor, Kathleen, Jason, Wren, Von, Verne, Alejandro, Billy, Priscilla, Jessica, Louise, Tanya C., Andy, Michelle, Towana, Kim, Charles, Jane, Mette, Amanda, Ann, Andrea, Margaret, Debbie, Beth, Carolyn, Rich, Andrew, Alexandra, Eileen, Jess, Lisa, Gail, Mat, Connie, Lois and many others who read, listened and cheered this book to completion.

65038051R00106

Made in the USA
San Bernardino, CA
26 December 2017